Versus

FSF Writers Alliance Anthologies, Volume 1

The Fantasy & Sci-Fi Writers Alliance

Published by The Fantasy & Sci-Fi Writers Alliance, 2024.

VERSUS

First edition. January 15, 2024.

ISBN: 979-8223183488

Written by The Fantasy & Sci-Fi Writers Alliance.

Thank you to all the members of the Alliance who contributed to this anothology, volunteered their time to the cause, and put their hearts on the line when they submitted stories to the contests.

None of this is possible without you.

Foreword by Jade C Wildy

Throughout the ages, humanity has fought for survival. Each rotation of our planet brings new challenges, as our world changes and evolves. For humankind to survive, we must adapt and learn. Deep down in the pit of our existence, we crave stories that will let us live out conflicts without coming to harm. We want to know who won the fight. We want to know who lost. We want to learn from all the mistakes made and consider how we ourselves might measure up. It's hardwired into our natures, just as much as we yearn for a good story. We thrive on conflict, intrigue, and mystery, and through these, we learn about ourselves and the world in which we live.

Stories that pit humanity against incredible situations allow us to live in realities beyond our imaginings while we discover things about ourselves and the world around us. Even the most far-reaching, fantastical tale has something to teach.

Drawing from the incredible global talent in the Fantasy and Science Fiction Writers Alliance, *Versus* presents thirteen stories that examine humanity's triumphs and failures in a world full of challenges.

Humankind competes with the demands of society, where the rigours of expectations take a toll on those of us who wish to go our own way and dare to be different.

> MJ James examines strict gender expectations and parenthood in a three-gender world where non-conformity is punishable by death in *The Act of Never Fitting In*.

In L.L. Baker's *A.R.C.,* the last surviving human, a girl, has the pressure of saving the world on her young shoulders until she discovers A.R.C. may be lying.

Radiation Days by E.B. Hunter shows us a changed world where a man grapples with the loss of his wife in the face of a conspiracy he never could have imagined.

Humankind comes up against the supernatural, examining questions of love, the balance of life and death, and what exists beyond our reality as we know it.

Kat Vancil's *The Mirror of Avarice* warps our reality when a man gets pulled into a Mirror Realm and meets a ghost who isn't, in fact, dead.

In *Chateau Mortem* by M. Fritz Wunderli a man goes to work at a retirement home. But he quickly learns the residents are elderly, immortal, and... dead.

G. Clatworthy's *Hell Hound of the Baskervilles* sees an agent with supernatural secrets get more than she expected when an urban legend about Hell Hounds turns out to be real.

Isa Ottoni's *Yours Truly* delved into the mysteries of the heart when a man is sent to interview a fairy.

Humankind's tumultuous connection with the technologies that infuse our daily lives has us asking if we trust them too much.

SR Malone examines our relationship with artificial humans and what happens when they start acting strangely in *The Intimacy Protocol*.

Nick McPherson questions if default programming is always the correct programming in *EXE.* where a robot decides how to function after a full system failure.

Drawing from Shakespeare, *Tomorrow, and Tomorrow, and Tomorrow* by EA Robins asks what will be left, where humans and machines alike, are all players upon the stage, pacing toward the end of recorded time.

Humankind faces off against their gods drawing from ancient mythologies, creating new imaginings of age-old tales of justice and when time is against us.

In M. Fritz Wunderli's *Chronoclysm*, the clock won't stop ticking and it seems everything stands in the way on a day when it's critical not to be late.

Dea Sulis Minerva by Isa Ottoni, sees two goddesses clash over a worship site and must decide what to do with a girl who has been wronged — abide by her request or curse her instead?

Set in 1970, *A Wrong Cruelly Done* by Michael C. Carroll reimagines Loki and the tragedy that instigates Ragnarok, retold in Belfast, Northern Ireland.

As humankind versus society, the supernatural, technology, and gods through each of these incredible stories, we see our own potential for triumph and failure reflected back. Humankind's survival relies on what we can learn, and what better place to learn than through the lens of the imagination of these talented authors?

Jade C Wildy holds degrees in visual arts, sustainability and writing, giving her a flair for culture. She returned to creative writing in 2020, concentrating on speculative fiction buJade C Wildy returned to writing in 2020, concentrating on speculative fiction, but branching out into fantasy, science fiction and horror.

She holds degrees in the arts and sustainability and writes on themes like death, psychological states, and being different. She believes in the power of storytelling as a motivator for change, and her writing has been included in numerous publications internationally.

A self-confessed wallflower, Jade lives in Australia and can be found writing or drawing in the local cafes.

www.jadewildywordsmith.com

This Anthology was edited by Aaron H. Arm.

Aaron H. Arm is a speculative fiction writer and freelance editor from central New York. His first novel, The Artifice of Eternity, was published in July 2023 by Cosmic Egg Books. Now, he spends most of his time editing other novels, memoirs, or anthologies. Aaron also has professional experience in technical writing, copywriting, mass communications, and teaching. He holds an MA in adolescent education from Ithaca College. You can follow his work at:

https://aaronharm.com

Section 1:
Gods
VS
Humankind

Chronoclysm by M. Fritz Wunderli

Chronoclasmic Compulsive Personality Disorder: A chronic, compulsive desire to destroy clocks or other timekeeping devices out of a mistrust of time and/or timekeeping devices, marked by delusions, anxiety, paranoia, and outbursts.

Victor looked at his alarm clock one more time. The red, digital numbers taunted him. He sat on the edge of his bed, still in his underwear and a white t-shirt. Sunlight spilled into the musty bedroom, catching dust particles hanging suspended in midair. He grabbed his round, thin-framed glasses from next to the clock and slipped them onto his face, pressing the nose pads firmly onto the bridge of his long, slender nose. He waited for the inevitable call. A cell phone sat on the bedside table. It suddenly started vibrating, emitting a low, monotonous hum.

Fuck, Victor thought as he reached for the phone. "Hello?"

"Victor, where the hell are you? You were supposed to be here twenty minutes ago!"

No shit. "Yeah, I'll be there soon. My alarm didn't go off."

"I have to leave in five minutes. If I'm late this time, I'm screwed. Got it? Marissa ain't playing anymore."

"I got it. I'll be there in fifteen. Just lock up before you leave." Victor stepped into his bathroom as he held the phone to his ear. He started peeing, the phone pressed to the side of his head with his right shoulder.

"The security update will be starting in twenty minutes. If you're late, and something happens, it ain't my fault. Got it?"

The security update would be automatic. Happened every day at the same time. "Yeah, yeah. I got it." He hung up and moved to the sink, where he brushed his teeth, applied copious amounts of deodorant, and tried to flatten his unkempt hair, still sticking out in odd angles. It would take him five minutes to get to the office. Another two to get through security and up the elevator. He'd pause for thirty seconds as he passed the project management cubicles to get a glimpse of Kat before shutting himself away in his office, where he'd stare at a screen for hours and answer calls from employees about how their computers weren't working.

He pulled on a pair of skinny jeans that were too short for him, buttoned up a short-sleeve shirt to the top, and slipped on a pair of birkenstock sandals. He grabbed his satchel from the back of his lone chair at the kitchen table and darted out of his studio apartment.

The bus arrived early. Silvie ran like an injured baby gazelle down the sidewalk, trying to keep balance while wearing high heels, waving her hand in the air to catch the bus driver's attention. Her brown leather purse swung wildly from the nook of her arm, and drops of her mocha frappucino spilled from the top of her Starbucks cup. The driver didn't stop. Silvie looked at her phone to make sure. It read 8:04 a.m. The 245 wasn't supposed to arrive until 8:10. She reached the bus stop and sat on the bench next to a gray-haired, shriveled old woman. Silvie set her purse and drink on the bench next to her and quickly adjusted her bra, stuffing her enormous breasts back into the cups. She brushed back her synthetic black hair, careful to keep her long, delicate fingernails from scratching her face or ruining her makeup.

Silvie noticed the old woman watching her. "Was that really the 245?"

"Oh yes, hun."

Damn, Silvie thought. "When's the next bus to 131st come?"

The elderly woman pulled out a small card from her clutch. It had the bus schedules printed out on a table. "The next bus going that way from here isn't until 8:45. You in a hurry?"

"I'm gonna be late for work," Silvie said irritably. She thought her options through and realized the only way to get to work on time was to call an Uber. She pulled out her phone and opened the app on her phone. "That's gonna cost me thirty-two bucks! Damn."

"Will you make it to work on time?"

Silvie nodded her head slowly, still staring at her screen. "This guy better hurry."

Sam poked his head out of his bedroom door and listened intently for any signs of life within the house. His parents should have been gone for work, but he wanted to be careful.

He strained his ears for any sounds that would indicate someone was moving around downstairs. Nothing but the normal creaks and groans from the old brownstone. He stepped out of his room and glanced down the stairs. No one. Just in case, he looked at the long table in the hall by the front door. There was a wooden bowl his mom had gotten when she and his dad went to Africa for a humanitarian trip two years ago. She now used it as a key bowl. Several keys were piled in the bowl, but—most noticeably—two sets of keys were missing: mom's Mercedes and dad's Audi.

Still in his boxer shorts and a dull gray hoodie, he walked downstairs and into the kitchen. It took him a second to realize he wasn't alone. His mom sat at the kitchen counter, a cup of coffee steaming in front of her as she poured copious amounts of creamer into the Columbian brew. She looked up and smiled, the same smile Sam recognized on all of the billboards and bus stop benches across the city. Her platinum blond hair bounced stiffly whenever she moved her head. She wore a charcoal gray pantsuit, making sure to wear her gold and silver bangles on her wrists, a gaudy diamond ring on her left hand, and a pearl necklace.

"Hey Sammy. You're up early."

Shit, Sam thought. He opened the fridge door, hiding behind it as he pretended to look for something to eat. Early? Did she say he was up early? He pulled out his phone from the hoodie pocket and looked at the lock screen. It read 8:22 a.m. Mom and dad always left by 8:15 like clockwork. They were predictable. He glanced at the clock on the oven. It read 8:07

a.m. He groaned quietly before pulling out the orange juice and shutting the fridge.

"Got any plans for today?" Mom asked.

"Nope."

"Well, try not to hang out on your computer all day. It isn't good for your eyes."

"Is Dad gone?"

"He had an early conference with some investors from Beijing. I'm leaving in just a minute. I'm showing a house up in Rochester today."

Sam didn't respond. He glanced at the oven clock again. 8:07. He sighed and drank his orange juice in a single gulp. "Cool. See ya."

"Hey, while you're on your computer, why don't you try looking up some jobs, or maybe classes at the university?" Mom called as he climbed back up the stairs to his bedroom. Sam rolled his eyes. College couldn't teach him anything he didn't already know or couldn't find on his own. He locked his bedroom door behind him and hopped into his bed. He pulled his laptop onto his lap and logged in. He was still early, but he figured it was worth a shot anyway.

Marvin held his breath and curled up in the corner of his room. His fingers plucked nervously at his eyebrows, pulling the hair out and leaving bald patches.

"You won't have any eyebrows left, Marvin, if you keep pulling your hair like that." A man in a tweed vest, corduroy slacks, and a pair of cracked leather loafers sat in a chair in the middle of the room. A clipboard rested in his lap. "Now, tell me what you think you heard last night."

The thoughts in Marvin's head were both fleeting and erratic, like lightning coursing through his brain, each vein a new thought that arrived and then disappeared just as quickly. He pulled his hands away from his eyebrows and sat on them to keep himself from tugging at his hair. "F-first, you have to get rid of it."

The man in the chair sighed. "You mean my watch?"

Marvin nodded vehemently, his thick brown curls bouncing.

"Fine." The doctor removed his watch and handed it to an orderly standing just outside the door.

The anxiety suddenly melted away, and Marvin's posture changed. He looked up at the doctor, who was patiently waiting. "Today. It'll happen."

"What will happen, Marvin?"

"There's no stopping it. Everything's already in motion. I heard it. I heard them talking."

The doctor sat forward. "Who was talking?"

Marvin retreated back into himself, curling into a ball and shivering. His fingers nervously plucked his hair at the back of his head. He mumbled unintelligibly, rocking back and forth.

"Marvin, who was talking? Did you hear someone say something?" the doctor pressed.

"The clocks. The clocks. They talk, talk, talk. The clocks are talking. Tick tock goes the clock, yes, it can talk. They plan and plot, nasty clocks. Tick. Tock. Tick tock clock."

"Marvin, we've been through this. The clocks can't talk."

"Oh they can talk, doc. The tick tock. They talk. They plot. Mischievous. Untrustworthy time. Unreliable, inconsistent, devious. Tick tock, tick tock. Yes, they talk. Just have to listen carefully."

"Okay, so what are they saying?"

"Money. Get the money. Take the money."

The doctor looked back at the orderly, who shrugged, just as confused as the doctor. "Is someone going to rob a bank, Marvin? Did you hear someone talking about robbing someone?"

"Not someone. No, not someone. Time. Time robs us all. Break the clocks. Break the clocks!"

The doctor sighed. "Alright, let's give him 2 milligrams of Ativan and see if that calms him down enough so we can talk. We aren't getting anywhere with him like this."

A broken bike chain lay on the sidewalk, still wrapped around the railing. Noticeably missing was his bike. It was nothing special, but Victor didn't have many possessions, and his bike was certainly one of the more expensive and useful things he owned. He looked at his watch. He had ten minutes to get to work. He could call a Lyft, but it would take several minutes for one to arrive and then several minutes more to get him there. On top of that, it would cost him money he didn't have. Walking was the only option.

He looked at his watch again. It was already 8:19, and the security update was scheduled to start at 8:30. It was important he made sure the security update started on time. He quickened his pace. Six blocks. That's all it was. He could do it. If he needed, he could start jogging, though he wasn't sure how fast he could run in birkenstocks.

Every thirty seconds, he'd look down at his watch. His pace was good. He could do this. Traffic was bustling, and every crosswalk swarmed with pedestrians. The city streets were always loud. Busses rumbled and screeched, taxis and rideshare cars zipped in and out of lanes, horns blared, engines backfired, construction crews contributed with a cacophony of drills, hammers, and cement mixers. Most everyone on the sidewalks were enmeshed in conversations on phones or rocking out to music on headphones. Little by little, Victor forced his way through throngs of distracted people. Every time he had to stop, he anxiously swayed from side to side.

Two more blocks. It was going to be tight, but he was going to make it.

Sam hadn't been on for more than five seconds when he got a private message. It was set to delete after two minutes. It was a number. The sender line was blank. Sam looked at the time. 8:21. The message was early. He smiled and committed the number to memory. He cracked his fingers and stretched them out to warm them up. He did a few practice lines on a blank document screen, testing how fast he could enter the number.

Time moved much more slowly as he kept an eye on it. Everything moved in slow motion. Nothing was going to distract him. He waited, poised to start like a runner waiting for the gun or a horse about to launch from the gate. It was a race, and so far, Sam had never won a race. He was always just too slow. But this time, he had a good feeling. He'd woken up early, and even though his mom was still home, it worked to his benefit. He would have missed the number, and that was a surefire way to lose from the start.

Silvie clambered into the back seat of the silver Ford Focus. The driver said hello and asked if she would like a drink of water or would prefer the windows down.

"No thanks. Can you get there before 8:45?"

The driver looked at the GPS on his phone. "That depends on traffic, but I think it's manageable."

"Thank you."

Before pulling away from the curb, the driver put on his blinker and patiently waited until a gap opened up in the steady current of cars. The driver was meticulous, making sure he followed every law, sticking to the speed limit, coming to a complete stop at every intersection before rolling through. Silvie's long fingernails drummed along the armrest. The caffeine was now starting to course through her veins. Her legs bounced anxiously. She watched as car after car passed by.

"I'm sorry, but can you speed up? I'm in a real hurry here."

"I'm sorry, ma'am, but I'm not allowed to go over the speed limit."

Damn, Silvie thought. The smell of coconut came from the air freshener hanging from the rear-view mirror. The seats had been recently vacuumed. In the pocket at the back of the driver's seat were pamphlets showing different things to do in the city, like museums, ferry rides, monuments to visit, and restaurants.

"Are you from out of town?" The driver asked, looking at Silvie through the rear-view mirror.

"Nope. Born and raised here."

"Oh, that's nice."

Silvie noticed the driver still looking at her.

"Can I ask what you do for work?"

"I'm a lawyer."

The driver's eyes went wide. "Really? Wow, that's a good job."

Silvie nodded, awkwardly avoiding looking into the rear-view mirror, where the driver's eyes were still looking at her.

"You know, I think I need to get a lawyer."

"Yeah?" Silvie responded half-heartedly. This always happened. It was one of the reasons she hated telling people what she did for a living.

"Oh yes. Maybe you could help me. You see, I have this cousin—"

Before the driver could go on, the car suddenly jolted, and a loud thump startled Silvie. She looked through the windshield only to see the hood dented on the front. Out of nowhere, a tall, thin man jumped up, limping on his left leg. His face was contorted in pain as he rubbed his thigh. The driver sat in shock for a moment before slowly unbuckling his seatbelt and getting out of the car.

This shit can't be happening right now. Silvie got out of the car. The man that got hit looked like one those software development nerds working for Google. She was surprised he didn't break anything. The guy looked like a twig.

"No, no, seriously, I'm alright. I really have to go."

"Sir, please, at least let me get your name and number. I have to write a report for this," the driver said. Silvie silently begged the driver to leave it alone so they could get going, but he was insistent. After several seconds of desperate begging, the man finally gave the driver his information before limping hurriedly away. This never would have happened if she had made it to the bus on time. She got back in the car as the driver returned. She looked at her phone. It was 8:23. She had twenty minutes and was still miles from the building.

The Ford Focus revved to life again with the driver muttering numerous apologies and explaining how that had never happened to him before. Silvie looked at the green numbers of the clock on the dashboard. It read 8:29. She checked her phone again. It read 8:23.

"Is that the right time?" Silvie asked, panic rising in her chest.

"Oh yes. Here, I have it on my phone as well."

Silvie glanced at his phone screen. In the top corner, in tiny numbers, the time read 8:29.

Agonizing pain ran through Victor's entire leg, radiating from the outside of his left thigh. Pressure sent shocks of electricity through his muscle. He hobbled the last block to his office building, working through the severe pain. Security let him through and he leaned against the wall of the elevator as it climbed to the eleventh floor.

Once the doors opened, he limped as fast as he could down the hallway. He pressed his access card against the sensor and waited for the lock to click before pushing into the room filled with servers. In the middle was a single computer on a desk. Victor sank into the chair and stared at the computer. The time was 8:32. The security update started at 8:31, sixty seconds late. Victor shook his head in disbelief as he scrambled to manually sift through every data access point to make sure there weren't any breaches. There were dozens. He combed through them, one by one.

Then he saw it. A single entry. At 8:30, sixty seconds before the security update began. One unauthorized user managed to hack the servers before the automatic renewal of security protocols could be implemented. Victor started to furiously purge the hacker, trying to kick him out of the system before too much damage could be done. Minutes passed before Victor could shut off access to the intruder. He sat back in his chair, breathing heavily, his leg throbbing. He needed to find out what the damage was. In the back of his mind, Victor knew he was fired.

Sam stared at the computer screen in disbelief.

What did I just do?

A private message popped up, sender line blank. "You win," was all it said. It vanished after thirty seconds. He looked at the time. 8:36. His phone vibrated next to him on his bedspread. It was his dad. He answered.

"Sam? Sam? Where are you?" Dad's voice sounded urgent, panicked.

"I'm at home. Why?"

"Did you get into our bank accounts?"

"What? No, of course not. What's going on?"

"Don't lie to me, son. If you needed money, you just had to ask."

Of course the asshole wouldn't believe me. "I didn't take shit. I'm still in my bed. What happened?"

There was a pause on the other end. "Everything's gone. All of it. All of our money is gone." The line went dead. Sam stared at the phone as the weight of what his dad said started to dawn on him. He looked from the phone to the computer screen, back to his phone.

What did I just do?

Marvin stared out his window over the grounds of the institute. Sprawling green lawns and a colorful garden with those little cherubic statues hiding behind rose bushes and under hedges. A handful of people were meandering the little gravel paths. His door was left ajar, but he preferred the indoors.

A commotion suddenly arose from the nurses station down the hall. Marvin poked his head out of his room to see several of the orderlies and nurses checking their phones or staring bewildered at their computers. Some looked shocked, others angry, a few were in tears. Marvin sighed and went back into his room and laid down on his bed. The Ativan was still pumping through his blood.

"Marvin? Marvin, sit up." The doctor had come in the room and stood over Marvin.

"What is it?"

"You knew, didn't you? You knew this was going to happen." The doctor looked both furious and confused.

"I don't know what you're talking about," Marvin said nonchalantly.

The doctor pulled out his phone and showed the screen to Marvin. On it was the doctor's bank account, the balance reflecting zero. "I had three thousand dollars in there this morning. Now it's just gone. And it isn't just me. Everyone who shared this bank now have nothing in their accounts. The money just vanished."

Marvin sat up and crossed his legs. "The money. Take the money. Get the money. Tick tock. Tick tock. That's what they meant."

"That's what who meant?"

Marvin looked up at the doctor. "The clocks."

Chronoclysm: Noun. A momentous, sometimes violent phenomenon caused by inconsistent fluctuations of time, which leads to a constellation of seemingly random events coalescing into overwhelming economic or societal upheaval and disruption.

Michael is, and always has been, in love with stories. Even as a lawyer, Michael attempts to merge storytelling with his practice. He has a BA in Creative Writing and is currently working on his first novel. He writes short stories in the meantime while juggling work, family, and the daily rigors of life. He lives in the shade of Mt. Olympus in Salt Lake City, Utah.

https://vocal.media/authors/m-fritz-wunderli

Dia Sulis Minerva by Isa Ottoni

Citizens of the Roman Empire flocked year-round to Aquae Sulis, a small town in the province of Britannia, to bathe in the sacred waters of the temple and plead their cases with Dea Sulis Minerva. Anyone who had been wronged could ask for revenge by writing their petitions on sheets of lead known as Curse Tablets and throwing them into the holy spring where the goddess dwelt. They did so eagerly and at their own peril.

In the centre of a parlour built of terracotta bricks and adorned with marble courses, Minerva sipped her golden wine, alone. She was used to the solitude, enjoyed it even, but for whatever reason, the silence fell heavier over the triclinium that day. Resting on a reclined couch, she glared at the mosaic walls before her, depicting the goddess and her famous victories: the judgement of Paris and the crumbling of the Trojan walls; the time when she beat her jerk of an uncle Neptune and won the city's patronage fair and square. Alas, that was such a long time ago. She even held a different name then.

Sighing, she sat up to refill her chalice of wine, the sweet smell filling the air. She'd better start working soon—the petitions would be accumulating already—but a headache threatened to spoil her day. Perhaps she should call Bacchus later. He had the best hangover cures. She lifted the chalice to her mouth, but as the liquid touched her lips, a call came from the hall: "Salvê, I'm home!"

Minerva gasped, wine pouring from her nose.

"Love, are you here?" the voice came louder—closer.

"In here!" Minerva called, wiping her chin and her amber-stained tunic. She chugged the rest of the velvet liquid before Sulis poked her head inside the parlour.

"There you are!" Sulis beamed, arms open as if meaning to embrace the world.

Minerva accepted the hug, doing her best not to look annoyed. Old gods could be so sensitive.

"I hope you had a good trip?" Minerva asked, pouring her partner a glass of wine.

"Oh, the best! I never knew the Dream Valley could be so ... dreamy!" Sulis sat on the couch opposite Minerva, her carmine hair bouncing about her fair complexion as she recounted the details of her journey.

An hour later, Sulis was still rambling about her holiday. "... Isis showed me around the underworld, and I met Pluto there—not a jolly fellow, is he? And—"

"Things around here are good too," Minerva interrupted.

"Oh, love, I'm sorry it took me so long to return. I hope the work was not too much?"

"No, love, not at all."

Sulis smiled, studying their surroundings: the grand parlour and its marble pillars, the vines growing to the ceiling, the statues, the mosaics, the feast presented before them. Her eyes widened in wonder. "Oh, my! Things have changed, haven't they? What have you been up to?"

"Not much, just caring for your site."

"Not much? Last time I was here we were nothing more than a bubbling brook. They built a Domus for us?"

"A temple." Minerva nodded. "And a bath."

"That's marvellous!" Sulis clapped excitedly. "And they've been worshipping us still?"

"Very much so, yes."

"Wonderful! Giving away many blessings, have you?"

"Erm ... yes, I guess you can say that."

"Oh, I'm glad." Sulis hopped to her feet. "Where are they? It's been a while, but I guess there is no better time to resume my responsibilities than now!"

"Down the hall, you'll find the spring and the curse —" Minerva cleared her throat " —the tablets in the water."

Grinning, Sulis scrambled out of the parlour. Minerva shook the last bottle of wine, cursing the little amount of liquid left. She should definitely call Bacchus. Sulis' sudden reappearance would surely worsen her headache and she'd better be prepared.

"Minerva!" Sulis' voice resonated from the hall. She marched into the parlour and dropped dozens of sheets of lead by Minerva's feet, her face wriggling in rage. "These are horrible!"

Minerva lifted her chalice in a mocking cheer. "Yep."

"How—How could they?"

"Humans are horrible." Minerva shrugged.

"No, no, no, you don't understand! Listen." Sulis picked a sheet from the ground and read it aloud. 'Dea Sulis Minerva, a lifetime of itching back, on a spot they can never reach, for stealing my mantle while I was in the bath.' Why would they pray for such an awful thing?"

"That one is kinda nice. An itching back is annoying, but at least it's not a bloody stool." Minerva shuddered. "That one was nasty."

"No!" Sulis cried. "How could you let things come to this? They used to pray for good weather and healthy crops and—"

"Ceres has those covered now."

"Oh ... well, love then, they could ask for true love!"

"That's Cupid's jurisdiction."

"Beauty?"

"Venus."

"Wealth?"

"Juno."

Sulis threw her arms in the air. "So we are left with these petty things?"

"Yeah ... I mean, we could call it justice. It sounds better than pettiness, I think."

"No, this is wrong, this is so wrong! How—"

"Listen, love." Minerva took Sulis's hands, squeezing them reassuringly. "You've been away for a while, so you're not in a position to complain. You said you needed a break, and I kindly agreed to help you out, so just ... chill. Here, have some wine. It will help."

Sulis accepted the chalice, defeat written on her face as she sank back onto the couch. She sipped the wine and picked another tablet. "This one asks for a year-round of nightmares for an insult."

"Hum ... spiders maybe? A couple crawling on their bed every night sounds fitting."

Sulis scowled before picking another one. "To murder the neighbour who deflowered their daughter."

"Ooh, murderers are expensive. We're sure to cash in big." Minerva scratched her chin. "How about stepping in a waterhole by mistake? No, better yet, cut their finger on a rose thorn and die of sepsis!"

"Minerva!"

"What?" Minerva patted the air. "I'm just brainstorming here."

Sulis shot to her feet, pacing around the younger goddess. "But what if the daughter wanted to be deflowered? What if the mantle kept the thief warm and safe at night? What if the insult was justified?"

"All right, I hear you," Minerva said, putting down her chalice. "We can shake things up a bit. It's not like we are wanting for money. How about we curse the curser instead? Make them pay for their pettiness?"

"We shouldn't be cursing people at all!" Sulis cried. "But also, we cannot go around indulging their every desire or they will never learn to be better."

"Ugh, you sound like Prometheus and his love for the creatures." Minerva leaned back on her couch, nursing the headache that pierced her temples. "He lost his liver for his kindness, but humans do not deserve it. You've just been away too long and forgot about it."

"Well, I'm back now. Let's go!"

Minerva's eyes shot open. "Go where?"

"To the Baths!"

Agnes stomped across the Temple complex, her grandmother Cassia in tow. Her light robes fluttered dramatically as she strode, her dark hair billowing in her wake. Aquae Sulis burst with activity, as citizens enjoyed the hot spring, pools, and exercise areas. Merchants cried as she passed by, offering all the goods one could ever want, but Agnes ignored them all. She had to find the spring where the goddess dwelt.

"Will you slow down!" her grandmother called, struggling to catch up with Agnes's purposeful steps. "My legs aren't what they used to be."

Agnes halted inside the hall of the Great Bath, a massive pool of hot healing water lined with forty-five sheets of lead—bigger versions of the one she clutched in her hand. The barrel-vaulted hall rose to the heavens, the largest building Agnes had ever seen, with walls painted scarlet and white, torches burning against pillars despite the natural light cascading from the high glass windows. Niches around the pool held benches and tables, where bathers ate and chatted, spying on those who chose to exercise and display their muscles and strength. Agnes took a deep breath. The hot vapours inside the hall were overwhelming. The scent of sulphur and sweat, revolting. The sheer number of people was staggering; Agnes wanted—needed—to get away.

"Ah!" Cassia said, joining her granddaughter. "Even the floor is heated! What a treat. After our sauna, we should take a bath in the caldarium and—"

"We're not here to enjoy ourselves," Agnes interrupted. "Now, where is the spring?"

"In the very heart of the complex, but—"

Agnes bolted away, anger rushing her steps. If nobody in this whole world would help her, Sulis Minerva would.

Minerva stifled a chuckle as Sulis marvelled at the structure built in their honour. The elder goddess gasped at every corner, praising the engineering and the beauty of their temple. She grinned in awe at the tiled mosaics depicting seahorses and dolphins, celebrated the imposing overarching roof, approved the steps leading into the water, and praised the ingenious plumbing and drainage channels toward the River Avon. Minerva had become somewhat desensitised to the place, but she found her partner's reaction to their worship site amusing.

"Do you think she looks like me?" Sulis asked, studying their gilt bronze statue inside the cellar.

"She has your eyes," Minerva said, "but my nose and brow. That helmet is unfortunate, though. It hides my best features." She pulled the elder goddess away from the temple, leading her into the Great Bath.

"Oh, they are so clever!" Sulis cried as her feet touched the heated floor. "And so pretty! Look at those bodies—so flexible and healthy! And so ... diverse!"

Unaware of the goddess gauging at them, a group of young men lifted weights by the pool, naked, dark skin gleaming with sweat. Sulis traced the lines of their torsos and backs with her fingers, eyes wide and mouth agape, before running to a group of women braiding each other's hair.

"You did a good job with these waters," Minerva said. "The spring provides good health and stamina, so they come from all over the empire. From the North, South, East and West, we are highly ... What was that word? Ah, democratic! The temple is always crowded like this."

"Indeed!" Sulis spun on her hills. "What else could they ever want?"

"Revenge, it seems." Minerva shrugged, plucking a chalice from a woman's hand. The woman carried on her conversation, oblivious to the theft.

"Right." A flick of anger crossed Sulis's eyes.

"So ... what's your plan, exactly?" Minerva asked, sipping the wine. Not as good as Bacchus's vintage, but it would do.

"Well, if I'm to curse people, I'll get the full story first."

"And if you disagree with the petition?"

"I'll curse them instead, as you said."

"Ooh, exciting!" Minerva pointed at a girl striding along the pool, an older woman in her wake. "How about her? She looks mad and ... Yep, she is definitely going for the spring."

Agnes's footsteps and heavy breathing were the only sounds breaking the silence in the heart of the temple. Contrasting with the other parlours, the spring gushed boiling water to an absent audience, steam and heat clinging to the marble walls. She knelt before the spring, on a circle of colourful mosaic depicting the goddess in her golden crown and spear.

Singing a prayer, Agnes swung the crumbled tablet over her head—but a calloused hand held her wrist, preventing her from throwing the curse into the water.

"Grandma!" Agnes cried.

"Shush! We're in a sacred place, no shouting in here."

Agnes tried to pull her hand free, but Cassia held her fast and forced her fingers open, snatching the tablet inside. Her eyes narrowed as she read the inscriptions. "Cursing him is not the answer."

"What is, then?" Agnes cried. "Nobody will listen to me—nobody! The curator, the master, Lord Callus, they say I could never have written the poem because I lack a fucking cock!"

Cassia chuckled, joining her granddaughter on the floor. "As if cocks could write anything, eh?"

"But I did write it," Agnes said, curling her hands into fists, eyes welling with tears. "That's my piece! And he—he stole it, that utter prick! Claimed my words as his!"

"I know, carissima." Cassia took her granddaughter's hands, massaging them open. "That was unfair, and you're right. But please, think before you do something you'll regret."

"I won't regret it, grandma, I swear I'll laugh as I watch him burn!"

Cassia sighed. "I would too if that made any difference. But even if Sulis Minerva heeds your plea—and she will, these waters are strong—what difference will that make? He'll be immortalised in the hall of poets, and you'll never get the recognition you deserve."

Agnes's chest tightened, her cheeks burning hot. She threw herself on her grandma's lap, who stroked her hair, soothing her as she wept. The curse tablet was her last option: the last chance of getting any sense of justice back. But now, even that was lost. Grandma was right. That prick dying wouldn't change those old farts' minds—they knew the truth already! Her heart hammered against her chest. She would never be published. She would never become the poet she knew she could become. "I worked so hard on that piece! Nights spent awake, hunting the old libraries, carefully choosing every single word and—"

"Listen." Cassia pushed her to a sitting position, lifting her chin so Agnes stared straight into her wrinkled eyes. "I'm not telling you to give up, just to ... be smart about it."

"How, grandma? How can I set things right?" Agnes sniffed, cleaning her nose on her tunic.

"Here." From her pocket, Cassia produced a brand-new sheet, gloriously blank. "We must always be mindful of what we wish for. Don't ask for specific things. Don't be stupid thinking you can choose the sentence to his crimes."

Agnes took the sheet with trembling hands.

"Tell the goddess what happened," Cassia said, "and let her weave his fate. She's a woman like us. She'll understand."

Minerva stared at the two women by the spring, mesmerised. The girl's petition ... It reminded her of past disputes against her brothers and uncles, and how even her father could be a jerk sometimes. Well, all the time, though seldom directed at her. But that was not it—not all of it. As she watched the old woman consoling the young one, shushing her sorrow away, a long-forgotten memory flared in her mind, of another desperate girl with the same dark wavy hair. Minerva had not been able to save her then—had failed to see Neptune's scheme and malice until it was all too late. Gorgo. The memory welled inside her heart, shame straining her chest, guilt burning behind her eyes.

"She worked so hard for the poem," Minerva breathed.

"She did." Sulis pushed herself out of the spring, splashing hot water on the mosaic floor. "What do you think we should do? Minerva?"

"Huh?"

"What do you think we should do?" Sulis repeated, handing over the retrieved tablet.

"Ah, yes." Minerva blinked, snapping out of her gloom. She read the inscription before crushing it in her fist. "We should burn him like she said."

"Are you crying?" Sulis asked.

"No! Of course not!" Minerva wiped her cheeks, turning her back to the elder goddess. "It's the steam and heat. Allergies. There's something in my eye."

"Aw, how sweet! Her prayer got to you, eh?"

"Stop it!" Minerva stormed out of the hall, climbing the steps back to the Great Bath. "It's just that I know what it's like to have your work undone by men."

"But you heard the lady: burning him will do no good."

"Maybe not, but I'd love to do it anyway."

"Why don't we burn his career and ego first?"

Minerva halted, causing Sulis to bump against her back. "What do you have in mind?"

Sulis tossed her red hair, an impish grin growing on her lips. "Oh, you'll see."

From all over the province, people flocked to the Temple, driven by an out-of-the-blue urge to bathe in the sacred waters. They marched into the Great Bath hall, some leaning shyly against the scarlet walls, some undressing boldly and diving into the pool. Everyone who was someone came to the baths that day. Everyone who might have been someone—given different circumstances—did too. Among the procession was the poet Titus and his retinue of lords and scholars.

"Ah, Lord Callus, what a great idea you had," Titus said, patting his companion on the shoulder. He flagged a servant and demanded a table. The boy ushered a group out of a nest to accommodate the famous poet and his crew. "Wine?"

Lord Callus nodded, leaning against his seat. Steam clung to his golden hair and skin, making him shine like a bronze sculpture. "I believe it was Master Chronicler who suggested coming here today."

"Oh, no," said the Chronicler, a stout little man. "Master Curator told me in the morning he meant to visit the baths."

"No, I didn't," said the Curator, scratching his balding head. "Titus was the one who invited me."

"Enough wine for you, my lords!" Titus's laugh echoed about the bath, resonating over the chattering and the splashing of water until it stopped abruptly.

Lord Callus followed his friend's frozen gaze, a grin creeping to his lips. Agnes stood on the opposite side of the pool, eyes locked with the poet, fury written on her face.

"What is it?" the Curator asked, squinting his eyes as he scanned the place.

"An unhappy lady," said Lord Callus. "She's been dealt with, Titus, so relax. She cannot hurt you."

"Lady Agnes is here?" asked the Chronicler. "Oh, poor thing. She looks most distre—"

Titus rose, bumping against the table and almost turning the chalices and jars in the process. He stood trembling for a beat of a heart before storming out of the nest. Moving oddly, as if his legs were forcing his will, he halted at the edge of the pool, staring at the lady on the opposite side.

"I ... ahem—" Titus cleared his throat. "I—" Something stuck inside his mouth, pressing against his tongue. "I—" he cried, his face red and sweaty. People noticed his odd behaviour, heads turning towards him. "I stole it!"

A heavy silence descended over the Great Bath. Lights dimmed down. From a high window, a lonely ray of sunshine washed over him. Like a play in an amphitheatre, Titus stood under the spotlight, all eyes on him. "I stole the poem Diana!" he bellowed. "Lady Agnes wrote it, but I called it mine!"

A second ray of sunshine lit Agnes as another character being introduced to the audience. She smiled, her face relaxed, eyes gleaming with pride. Beside her, another woman stepped into the light. Agnes took her hand.

"I stole Europe!" Titus cried, spit shooting from his lips. "Domitia wrote the poem, and I called it mine!"

"What are you doing, man!" Callus barked, pulling Titus by the arm.

Titus jerked his hand free, pushing Callus back. The lord fell over a table, and strong arms held him in place—strong dark arms of the young men who had been exercising by the pool.

"I stole Amatoria!" Titus cried. "Marcus wrote it, and I called it mine!"

Marcus, a young man with red curly hair, joined Agnes and Domitia. Then Albina and Mariana, as their names and poems were called, followed by Octavia, Felix, Antonia, Sirius, and Lucia. Titus's victims stood in line, hands clasped together, as the jury and witnesses to the poet's crimes.

"I stole from them all!" Titus's breath came in gulps of air. He pulled against his hair, clenched his teeth, trying to stop the words flooding from his mouth. Unhinged, he stripped off his tunic. Naked, he bellowed his confession. "I tried to write! I really did, but the muses never answered my call! My poems are broken! I'm an impostor! A fraud! But these people—half of them mere women, and the men, nothing but plebeians! Ha! They can write but they cannot publish! What an irony! I can publish! I published their work as mine!"

"Shut the fuck up, Titus!" Lord Callus pleaded against the arms holding him in place.

"Callus knew!" Titus cried, pointing an accusing finger. "The Curator and the Chronicler knew! They were complicit! They helped ... they ... they—"

Light flooded the parlour as the spell broke off. The chattering of the crowd began anew, eyes glaring at the naked not-a-poet as curses flew in the air. People booed.

"Bastard!"

"Coward!"

"Cheap crook!"

An elder lady threw a ripe plum at Titus; the fruit bounced off his head, tainting his face with red juice. Cabbages followed, grapes and figs plumbing down the man. Titus ran. A servant boy flipped a jug of wine over his torso, boos and curses trailing in the wake of Lord Callus, the Curator, and the Chronicle—the crowd chasing them out.

"Well done!" Minerva lifted her chalice, saluting the elder goddess. She watched Agnes embrace her new friends, cheering with the crowd who patted their backs and shook their hands. "What now?"

"Well, see that old man by the pool?" Sulis asked. "He is in charge of the library. Due to the sheer number of witnesses—important ones, too; I summoned everyone who was someone here today, including a Tribune from Londinium—he'll have no choice other than to give credit where credit is due. The girl and the other poets will have the recognition they deserve and that'll set a precedent for generations to come."

"He doesn't look very happy," said Minerva, eyeing the old man's scowl. "But I'll make sure he follows your plan." She waved her hand at him. "A nightmare a night until he sets things right."

Sulis chuckled. "You and your curses."

Minerva waved at a servant. The boy refilled her chalice as if she were just another visitor and not the goddess in charge. Sulis took a chalice of her own before the boy wiggled away. Arm in arm, they bathed in the joy their curse had woven.

"Thank you," came a voice from behind.

Sulis and Minerva turned. Before them stood Cassia, the girl's grandmother, beaming with pride.

"She can see us?" Sulis whispered. "Like, really see us?"

"I think she can," Minerva muttered.

Cassia kissed each of the goddesses' hands before joining her granddaughter for a hug.

"You know what, Sulis?" Minerva said, "You were right. Getting to know these humans before we curse them was a great idea. I believe ... I'll keep this up."

"We'll keep this up, love." The goddesses clinked their chalices together. "Make sure they get what they deserve."

Isa Ottoni (she/her) writes fiction with a spark of magic and fantasy with a spark of reality. When Isa is not writing, she is teaching and putting her PhD in food consumption sciences to good use, even though she would much rather be writing or reading about — you guessed, magic. She believes fantasy is what makes life fun, and that is a hill she is ready to die on. Isa was born and raised in Brazil but moved to Portugal seeking a new adventure. She lives with her incredibly supportive husband and their dog, a mischievous little mutt who thinks himself the king of everything that light touches. Isa doesn't have the heart to contradict him.

https://isaottoniwrites.wixsite.com/website

A Wrong Cruelly Done by Michael C Carroll

"An arrow from a horned bow, missed the mark and shot his kinsman, one brother the other, with a bloody dart. That was an expiable killing, a wrong cruelly done."

—Beowulf, lines 2437-2441

Belfast: December 10th, 1971

The flames in the Belfast pub's fireplace flickered with each opening of the tavern's door. Northern Ireland's most decorated officers hung from portrait frames on the tattered walls while the dim lamps guarding the room's perimeter cast their dull beams across the floorboards. Throughout the bar, cigarettes balanced on ashtray rims, their smoke billowing toward the ceiling like a dozen funeral pyres, drifting skyward before seeping into the overhead panels.

The young Irishman standing by the bar reached into his trousers to retrieve his wallet. With fingers still stiff from the cold, it took all his dexterity to pry open the folds. A disheartened expression consumed his face. No glimmering coins glowed within, no identification card declaring his name, no banknote clean or crumpled. Only a book of matches stared back from the leathery depths. Accepting that the whiskey he desired was not a feasible option, the Irishman plucked from his jacket a pouch of hand-rolled cigarettes.

His whiskey would have to wait until his brother's arrival.

Pushing back his sleeves, the Irishman reached for an unoccupied ashtray. With the northern statesmen scowling from their frames above, he unfastened the pouch and gazed upon the finest cigarettes Peterson's Dublin storefront could offer. They were stunningly precise. Each adhesive seal as straight as an arrow. Each tube a perfect replica of its brethren. Each cylinder aligned dutifully at attention. All save one.

One rolled cigarette faced the opposite way: the rebel cigarette, a superstition he and his brother upheld since their days lifting packs from the Dublin marts. With every pouch they rolled, they flipped a cigarette. As the years passed, his brother's time living north of the border made him partial to the sweeter tobacco of Murray and Sons, but despite their brand preferences, the brothers always smoked the rebel cigarette last. It was more than a good luck charm. It was a reminder that someday their souls would spill skyward from their lungs and ascend to taverns unknown. His rebel cigarette would stand guard, protecting that pouch until the day he died. His brother's would do the same.

Glancing around at the flags that filled the Belfast pub, with their red crosses and their red hands beneath their red crowns, the Dubliner felt not unlike that rebel cigarette.

What would the bartender do if he overheard their plans? How might those framed statesmen respond if they heard his Nationalist heart pounding beneath his sweater? Would they have him tied to a prison post?

The bells tethered to the pub door snapped the Irishman from his trance. He knew without turning who had entered. There could be no mistaking that off-key whistling of "The Foggy Dew." A thin smile spread across the Dubliner's face as his older brother clasped a firm hand on his shoulder and pulled back the stool alongside him.

***

Jostling the cubes of his whiskey glass, the Irishman donned his coat and glanced around the closing tavern. Like the flames from the fireplace, the lamps that lined the walls flickered and went dark. The light-haired gentleman who had assumed the nearest barstool had already flung his scarf around his neck and left through the tavern door. A stream of inky liquid trailed across the wet bar where the server must have retrieved his brother's bill. All that remained upon the bar top were the Irishman's gloves, a set of damp coasters, and his brother's cigarette pouch, precious property he promised to guard while his brother finished in the bathroom.

After his final sip, the Dubliner plunged his hands into his gloves and looked toward the bathroom door for any sign of his brother. They had entered separately, and while he wished to bid his accomplice farewell, it was more important that they not be seen leaving together.

That was when he heard the oak door chime.

Like water spewing through a narrow hose, a steady stream of Guarda spilled across the tavern's threshold. The young Irishman only had time to grab his brother's cigarettes before the firm glove of a Northern Irish policeman seized him by the collar and flung him to the ground. With his cheek pressed against the Guinness-soaked floorboards, the last thing the Dubliner saw was a gigantic officer kicking through the door to the bar's water closet.

Belfast: December 11th, 1971

From the sparse beams of light penetrating the cloudy window of his cell, the Irishman could not decipher the hour when he awoke. Far more tangible than the time, however, were the bruises that darkened his cheeks. His mouth tasted of iron; a bloody stream trickled from his molars, forming a sticky pool beneath his tongue. Touching his cheek, a jolt of sharp pain engulfed his face. He cringed as he remembered how the Guarda officer had thrust his jaw into the shards of his whiskey glass on the tavern floor.

Despite his pain, the Dubliner was already deciphering what had happened. Which tavern goer had overheard their conversation? Was his brother nursing wounds in an adjacent cell? Would this derail their plans? The Dubliner deemed these riddles unsolvable without the aid of cigarettes.

The clang of keys at the cell door interrupted his musings. When the iron hinges creaked open, a tall man stepped through the entrance. The Irishman kept his focus upon the concrete floor; before long, however, he allowed his gaze to travel from the man's pristine leather shoes up his trousers to his tidy, tweed overcoat. The Irishman's first impression was that the man seemed like a figure transported from a distant past, from some other world or history. The mysterious man tucked his wool cap under his arm and opened a manila folder.

"I suppose I should begin with an introduction." The tall man ran a hand through his blonde hair. "Good morning, sir. My name is Louis. Detective Louis. I'm assigned to your case."

The Irishman said nothing.

Detective Louis peered at the prisoner over the top of his folder and calmly retrieved a document before speaking again. "Before we continue, you should know that I'm not affiliated with the Northern Irish Government. Nor am I associated with the Irish Republic. I was born in Sweden."

Still, the Irishman said nothing.

"Belfast keeps a few of us ... northerners on retainer for special cases. You and your brother represent the kind of puzzle I tend to solve. Cases of unknown identities. I believe you Irishmen would refer to them as a 'Sean Doe,' would you not?"

The exhausted Dubliner bit the corner of his lip to keep from smiling. Cases of unknown identities. Their names remained a mystery.

Retrieving a slip from the manila file, the detective pulled a pair of thin-framed glasses from his pocket. "Judging from your tranquility, I assume you will have no issue with me reading the transcript of your arrest from last night?"

The Irishman dropped his gaze back to the concrete floor and remained silent.

"Excellent." Detective Louis held the parchment to the light that spilled from the cell's window, "December 10th. Two Irish males. Approximate Age: 25. Both men had medium build and short, dark hair. Neither criminal held identification papers." The investigator lowered the transcript. "Criminal? That's a bit harsh, don't you think?"

The Dubliner was too headstrong to take the bait; nevertheless, he appreciated the detective's empathetic tone.

"Record of arrest," Detective Louis continued. "Belfast officer: 'Sir, you are under arrest. Put the glass down and put your hands behind your back.'"

The detective was enjoying the charade. "Alright. Sounds reasonable. You replied with ... 'Get your Tanny hands off me, you loyalist bastard.' Hmm. Eloquent."

The transcript somehow reinvigorated the wounds on the Irishman's cheek.

"Oh, excellent, there's more on the back!" The detective turned the page with a dramatic furl. "Belfast Officer: 'We will use force if you act belligerently.'

"To which you responded ... 'Eat shit, you copper prick.'" The detective smiled, "That one has a nice ring to it."

"'Criminal was then lowered from his barstool to the floor.' Bit of a euphemism there...ah, yes. But here we are. The final act. The denouement." He read on, "'Belfast Officer: 'Where's your brother?' You replied...'Get your hands off me, you throne-worshiping fuck!' "

"Bravo. Magnificent. A masterpiece. Paints quite the picture, doesn't it?" Neatly tucking the paperwork into the folder, Detective Louis sat upon the untouched sheets that covered the inmate's bed.

"Look," the investigator said rubbing his brow thoughtfully, "I've been in this business a long time. As the years have passed, I've found myself caring less about the people and more about solving these riddles, you see? So this may come as a surprise to you—but I don't really care about you or what flag you salute."

The stark confession caught the Irishman's attention like a hook ensnaring the lip of trout; the Dubliner propped his back against the wall and dabbed the wound on his cheek contemplatively.

Tapping his manila folder, the detective continued, "I don't take every case Belfast sends my way. There needs to be something that impassions me. And what I find most intriguing about your case is the statistics. Let's take a look ..."

Nudging his glasses up his nose, the detective plucked a fresh sheet from his folder:

"September 19th: Car bomb, Finnegan's Pharmacy, Casualties: Zero. Injured: Zero.

- "October 5th: Car bomb, Oisin's Tavern. Casualties: Zero. Injured: Zero.

- "November 1st: Car bomb, Donegal Street Thrift Store: Casualties: Zero. Injured: Zero.

"November 28th: Car bomb, O'Connor's Jewelry: Casualties: Zero. Injured: Zero.

"Four explosions in the past three months. Before each explosion, the shop owners received a sprig of mistletoe in an envelope. After each explosion, dozens of witnesses reported a masked man clearing the streets prior to the blast. Each explosion completely decimated a known Loyalist business. Yet, the explosions left nobody harmed. Not one casualty. Quite impressive."

Detective Louis snapped his glasses shut and slid them into his coat pocket. "These 'Mistletoe Brothers'—that's what they've been deemed by the Belfast papers—seem to me more like patriots than vigilantes. And were you to ask me what I thought about their casualty-free, revolutionary cause? I'd say that throughout what feels like centuries of cases, I might have found a pair of like-minded souls. I think we should be asking how we could make these brothers more comfortable," and, after a pause, he added, "more like the heroes I believe them to be."

When the investigator stood to his towering height, the Irishman thought the Swede must have come from a line of mythological giants. The Dubliner stood to meet the detective's calculated stare.

After a long exhale, the detective turned to leave but stopped when he heard the Dubliner's voice: "Cigarettes."

"Pardon?" His position kept the prisoner from seeing the smile that spread across his face.

In a voice worn raw with clotted blood, the Irishman spoke, "You asked what could make those brothers feel more comfortable. Cigarettes. Bring the pouch of cigarettes from my jacket the night of the arrest. The Murray and Sons pouch. Give me a cigarette, and I'll consider talking with a fellow revolutionary."

Detective Louis gave the Irishman a nod before setting the lock and disappearing into the darkness.

Belfast: December 18th, 1971

"Come along now, I've visited enough this past week for you to know I would ask."

The Irishman kept his attention in his lap. While he enjoyed the investigator's visits, whenever Detective Louis was present, a nervous sensation overtook the Dubliner's body.

"Look," the investigator said as he plucked a page from his folder, "I'm more interested in solving your case than I am punishing a pair of brothers with political leanings not far from my own. Why don't I simply tell you what I've deduced? Don't say anything. Just keep puffing on that cigarette. Sound like a plan?"

The Irishman said nothing.

"Excellent." The detective rubbed his palms together enthusiastically. "I'll take your silence for begrudging compliance. Let's see here, where to begin? I suppose we should start where the Belfast Guarda gave up, shouldn't we?"

"Poor lads packed it in when your file came back empty," the detective addressed the Irishman, but his attention remained on the file. "No ID, no residential records, no medical history. Not so much as a dentist appointment anywhere from Donegal to Cork. Nothing. But while Belfast's finest took those absences as reason to throw away the case, I drew a different conclusion. You're orphans."

Not wanting his expression to reveal his shock, the Irishman scratched his chin inquisitively.

Pacing the small cell, the detective pointed with his pen to the plate of scraps by the door. "I've noticed that every time I visit, you leave your potatoes untouched. Strange habit for an Irishman. Until you consider how often the Republic orphanages serve potatoes. Makes sense. Abundant, simple to prepare. But I imagine a pair of teenagers growing up in Dublin group homes would have tired of the national delicacy, right?" The detective knew he was right.

"Now the fun begins. Where do these mysterious Mistletoe Brothers reside?" He continued without giving the prisoner time to respond. "Admittedly, this had me stumped. But that was before I realized I needed to consider multiple locations."

"These" the investigator tossed the sealed pack of Peterson's hand rolled cigarettes into the Irishman's lap, "can only be purchased in Dublin, while these," his brother's Murray and Sons pouch thudded on the prison floor, "are only sold on the Belfast docks. Interesting. Our beloved Mistletoe Brothers live in different cities."

"Which explains a lot," Detective Louis said as he continued pacing, "because even the most-inept policemen would not let that many vehicles and that much gunpowder go unreported. Which presented the question of how you acquired the materials in the first place. For that, we turn to the docks."

It was like watching a prodigious midfielder dribble across the pitch. Every decision was calculated. Each movement performed with precision. Every breath served a precious and secret purpose.

"If you can believe it, your gloves gave this one away." Detective Louis tucked his folder under his arm and looked intensely at his upturned hands. "The gloves you wore the night of your arrest were torn across their palms, rubbed thin by thick docking ropes. Incredible. But that wasn't the best part. Embedded in the wet cloth of those gloves, I found tiny, dark grains. Gunpowder."

All the Irishman could do was stare in awe. The Detective had methodically unraveled the tangled coil he and his brother had spent years binding. Shaking his head with disbelief, the prisoner could only listen and learn how far the investigator had traveled down their carefully constructed rabbit hole.

"That was my favorite part." The detective pretended not to see the Irishman's incredulous expression. "Repurposed British gunpowder. Car bombs born from loyalist ingredients. You were blowing up Belfast with their own damn explosives!"

"And for your grand finale," the detective's voice rose triumphantly, "you used German vehicles. Fresh off the boat from Berlin. Your brother illegally parked them and had them towed from the Belfast docks. Once they went unclaimed—because, well, nobody owned them—he paid for their rescue from the junkyard. I found an expired parking slip in his trousers.

"Incredible," the detective said, "I knew the Mistletoe Brothers would not disappoint ... but the riddle is not yet solved."

The detective's voice suddenly became serious. The Irishman inhaled sharply, trying not to show his nerves. In a flash, the Swede's glare turned insatiable, its wrath piercing, his manners terrifying. The Irishman trembled.

Then Detective Louis breathed deeply and smiled at the prisoner. His ferocity vanished; his placid demeanor returned. With a snap of his reading glasses, the investigator sighed. "Well, despite all of that, three facts still elude me: the identities of these mistletoe brothers, their upcoming targets, and their method of communication. Now, I know you'll never reveal your brother's identity," the detective admitted, "but if I were to guarantee your release by Christmas for providing any pertinent information, would you reconsider complying?"

The young Irishman peaked down at his brother's pouch of rolled cigarettes on the prison floor and saw the rebel cigarette staring back. The Irishman shook his head.

"Very well then." The investigator sported a mischievous grin. "The game persists."

Long after Detective Louis latched the door, the Dubliner could hear the hiss of the investigator's final word reverberating from the walls of his cell.

Belfast: December 24th, 1971

The Irishman could not tell whether it was dawn or dusk when he awoke to the sound of Swedish footfalls. Something about Detective Louis's gait did not feel right. When the investigator entered the cell, he seemed uncharacteristically disheveled. Whatever news he had could not wait.

"Sorry for the early visit," the detective exhaled to gain his composure, "but there's been a development in your case."

Sitting upright, the Dubliner rubbed his brow. The feeble rays that spilled from the foggy window indicated that the sun had not yet risen.

"I'll get right to the point." Another long breath. "Despite the patriotic silence you have upheld, your brother has had a change of heart. In exchange for his release, he agreed to reveal your identities." From his folder, Detective Louis pulled a single sheet of paper.

"That's impossible," the Irishman's voice croaked with skepticism. Dragging his legs to the edge of the cot, he reached for the document. Pinched between the detective's finger and thumb was the pouch of Murray and Sons hand rolled cigarettes. The Dubliner found that his taste had changed in favor of his brother's brand ever since his imprisonment.

"It's true. At this moment, your brother's meeting with the Belfast police. They are arranging the terms of his release. The document in your hand was drafted last night by the commissioner himself and initialed by your brother shortly thereafter. Look for yourself at the bottom. I believe you'll recognize your brother's hand."

The detective paused. "I'm sorry to bring you such unfortunate news." He could not look at the Irishman. A forlorn expression covered his face.

As the Dubliner examined the file, the world around him changed. The sparse rays of light from the rising sun seemed to darken and fade. The concrete walls surrounding him felt cold and thick. Somewhere beyond the muddy cell window, a crow barked and sang. The detective's voice grew indecipherably muffled, like the words of an important sermon heard underwater. The Dubliner stared at what was undeniably his brother's signature at the foot of the page: the letters C and D with a sword underneath raining droplets of blood from the hilt.

"As the lead investigator on this case—and an admirer of a devoted patriot—I think it best that I explain your options." The investigator slid to the floor. The Dubliner nodded his head but said nothing. His attention remained fixed upon the initials carved like a scar upon the page.

"This file diminishes your leverage, but you can walk free if you reveal your brother's identity along with any information pertaining to future explosions. Your brother, for whatever reason, was unable or unwilling to disclose those plans. But any deal to be offered must be made immediately. Once your brother exposes you, which that document states he will, my hands will be tied."

The Irishman said nothing.

"Look..." The detective lowered the document the Irishman clutched. "Over these past three weeks, I have come to admire your tenacity. But more than your rebelliousness, I have come to respect your unwavering dedication to your brother. That is a love I will never know. But I can tell you with absolute certainty that if you don't reveal his identity, they'll have you killed. They'll drag you down that forsaken hall, they'll tie you to that post—right there in the courtyard—and they'll fill your chest with enough bullets to stop your patriotic heart. I, for one, do not want to see that happen."

"What should I do?" For the first time since he took his brother's confession, the prisoner lifted his attention from the signature seared upon the document. His hands shook as he lowered the paper. Tears soaked the rims of his eyes.

"Ultimately, that decision is yours." The detective rose to leave. With his hand poised on the door, he stopped. The light from the murky window illuminated a Swedish flag tattooed on his forearm. "Were you to ask me—not as a detective, but as a friend—I would suggest that you give them the information. Your brother made his choice. You can clearly see where his allegiances reside. Choose life, Dubliner, and keep that rebel heart beating. There's no limit to what a passionate heart can do. Your brother lost sight of that. Don't succumb to the same fate."

"Wait."

Detective Louis' hand was on the latch when the prisoner spoke.

Without saying another word, the Irishman opened his brother's pouch of rolled cigarettes. From his lap, the rebel cigarette peered back at the Dubliner proudly. Taking the delicate paper, the Irishman held the cigarette up to the dull morning light. He stared in silence.

In the years that followed, the Irishman would have trouble explaining what he was waiting for in that moment. Was he waiting for his brother's initials to somehow un-sign that wretched sheet? Was he waiting for some acknowledgment, some confirmation, that he was making the right choice in betraying his kith and kin? If he ripped apart that paper, might it undo the damage they had done? If he held that cigarette to the light of the sunrise long enough, would the bagpipes that bellowed the bars of "Danny Boy" begin to play?

Then, like a seasoned fisherman gutting his midday catch, the Irishman sliced his thumbnail beneath the adhesive seal that bound his brother's rebel cigarette. Tobacco spilled across the young man's lap, dusting the prison floor. With the coiled casing writhing in his hand, the Dubliner smoothed the thin sheet against his knee. He did not need to check the paper to know what secrets that cigarette held. They were the same secrets he had written the night of their arrest. The same secrets he and his brother swore they would go to the grave protecting. The same secrets that would cost his brother his life.

His face unable to mask his astonishment, Detective Louis took the sheet from the prisoner and tilted the small page toward the window:

January 3rd, Murphy's Provisions, 5:20 pm

February 18th, Cullen's City Market, 9:05 am

March 15th, Derry Street Pub, 11:10 am

In the corner of the sheet, the Irishman had signed the letters B and D. Below the prisoner's initials, the investigator could see the faded image of a bow and arrow; a stream of blood dripped from the barb.

"As orphans, we chose our own names." With a shaking hand, the Dubliner pointed to the affidavit his brother had signed. "Claiomh. That's Irish for sword." Then he pointed to the unfurled cigarette. "Bougha. Irish for bow."

"And the surname?" The detective's voice seeped with pity and admiration.

"It's draped across the hilt and arrowhead," said the Dubliner on the verge of collapse. "Hanging from each is a sprig of mistletoe. Drualus. Irish for mistletoe. Bougha and Clajomh Drualus. Bo and Clay, for short."

"Unbelievable," whispered the detective under his breath.

"Now, please, detective, if you don't mind giving me the cell for a moment." Bo Drualus peered out the clouded window at the prison yard post.

"Of course, Mr. Drualus. I'll run my report. Let's see if I can hold up my end of the deal."

The Irishman peered out the window.

It was not until the detective had mournfully closed the cell behind him that the Dubliner turned from his courtyard vigil. "Detective Louis?"

Footfalls returned from the hall. "Yes, Bo?"

"You've learned my surname, but I don't know yours."

A long silence from the corridor. Then, from the darkness, the detective's answer: "Keye. Louis Keye. But those who know me well call me Lo."

And the detective was gone.

Belfast: December 25th, 1971

The rattle of cups and plates against the iron bars of the prison hallway arose Bo Drualus from his shallow slumber. Sleep never came easily to the Dubliner; now he doubted he would ever sleep peacefully again. The shouts of the Belfast inmates grew louder with each passing moment. Evident from their labored exclamations, a set of guards appeared to be dragging a prisoner down the corridor very much against his will. Bo peered out of his cell for a closer look. It was then that he saw his brother's face for the first time since their arrest.

"Get your fuckin' hands off me!" Clay Drualus barked as the guards jerked the furious combatant down the hall.

"Clay! Can you hear me? Clay!" In an instant, the Irishman's wounds of betrayal vanished. His brother needed him.

"Bo? For the love of God! Is that you?" Like a child waking from a nightmare, Clay Drualus spun in the dimly lit hallway in search of his brother. Spotting Bo's face, Clay flung himself toward the cell with enough force to dislodge the three guards ushering him down the corridor.

When the sentinel grabbed his shoulder, Clay turned to him with fire blazing in his eyes. Venom dripped from his lips: "That man is my brother! You aren't worthy to tie the laces of his fuckin' shoes. If you don't remove your bloody hands and let a condemned man talk with his brother, I swear by whatever gods you worship north of the border, I will come back as a ghost and haunt these fuckin' halls until the day you die!"

With a begrudging groan, the guard lifted his hand and let the Mistletoe Brothers speak.

"You look like shit, Bo," said Clay through a smile wet with crimson blood.

Bo had trouble formulating his frantic thoughts. As a result, all that spilled from his throat were questions. "Clay, what happened? What have they told you? Where are they taking you?"

Despite the circumstances, Clay had a smile on his face. "I suppose they're bringing me to join our rebel pals at the Far Away Pub." He added with a wink, "Don't worry, I'll start us a tab."

Bo felt the muscles that lined his jaw tighten. He swallowed hard. Tears pooled beneath his eyes. "I'll fix this, Clay. Just give me another day. I'll talk with Detective Lo. I'll figure it out."

A gash on his forearm reopened when Clay tightened his grip on the iron bars. "There's nothing else to be done, Bo. My jig is up. You pour one out for me each Christmas morning, you hear? When you're old and fat and happy. You tell that sweet wife of yours, whenever you meet the poor lass, that your brother was the bravest of the brave. You tell those kids when you have 'em how their Uncle Clay fought those throne-bowing pricks until the bitter end. Alright?"

"Clay, why did you do it?" Bo's voice cracked. Tears soaked his face. "Why did you sign the sheet? If either of us was going to cave, I thought for sure it'd be me. Why, Clay? Why did you—"

"They forged it, Bo. The blonde bastard sitting alongside us at the bar. That tall fella with the Swedish flag on his forearm. He lifted my bill when I hit the loo. Probably called the alarm himself. They pulled my initials from that soggy old bar slip." Clay chuckled. "You always told me that the drink would be my undoing. I guess you were right."

Bo's gaze dropped to the floor. "Clay, then it was me. I was the one—"

"I'll hear not another word of it." Clay lifted his brother's drooping chin through the bars with one hand and shoved away an approaching guard with the other. "Forget it. Fuck 'em. You get yourself out of here, do you hear me? And you forget the whole fuckin' thing. You get out of here and you live. Don't you ever dip your hand in a barrel of gunpowder again." He added with a wink, "If you do, when I'm done haunting this fat pig, you're next."

In a blur, the guards were on him, wrestling Clay into submission and dragging him toward the door at the end of the hall. Still clutching the iron bars of the cell, Bo cried into the hollow belly of the Belfast prison. It was not a cry for help. It was not a cry of desperation. It was a lamenting cry, a defiant cry, the cry of a rebel.

"Detective Lo! How could you, Detective Lo? Detective Lo Keye!"

Clay's howl grew softer with each step that carried him away from his brother. "Get your hands off me, you Tanny piece of shit! 'O Danny boy! The pipes, the pipes are—' "

The door at the end of the prison hall slammed shut.

With a B.A. Degree from Boston College and an M.A. from the Bread Loaf School of English, Michael C. Carroll specializes and lectures on literature from the Anglo-Saxon era, specifically the epic poem of Beowulf. His Master's program brought him to Oxford University where he studied Old English and the Beowulf Manuscript with Oxford professor and author Francis

Leneghan. The thesis that he wrote for the program became a 150-page book that explores the climactic dragon fight that concludes Beowulf. Michael C. Carroll has a passion for literature, a deep understanding of the Old English source material at the heart of my writing, and a love for grammatical editing born from ten years of teaching.

https://www.instagram.com/michael.c.carroll/

Section 2:
Technology
VS
Humankind

The Intimacy Protocol by SR Malone

Thick grey clouds were moving into view as Lori Lucero pulled into her street, the SUV moving silently like a bird of prey. She brought it to a halt outside number fifteen Ashwood Lane, taking a moment to compose herself.

She removed her shades and flicked down the driver-side vanity mirror. A combination of eyeshadow and jet lag marred her weary eyes.

Number fifteen appeared undisturbed, like the rest of the houses on the block. And, like the rest of the homes here, it was dotted on all sides by saplings and the occasional grand oak. A Unified Earth flag flapped in the breeze atop its pole. Stirring clouds darkening the approach to the house as Lori waited on the porch, fishing for her keys.

Even if Ed is in, he'll have the doors locked, she thought. Sure enough, the front door was locked, a heap of keys jammed in the opposite side. Over the last thirteen years together, including their nine years of marriage, Lori had picked up on every idiosyncrasy that formed the makeup of Ed Lucero, locking the doors for fear of burglars being one of the front runners.

She rang the doorbell, and, sensing movement amongst the dark shapes inside, craned her neck beyond the porch to see in the window.

Within seconds, the door was pried open.

"Greetings. May I help you?"

Lori's mouth hung open, visible confusion on her face. "I live here. You're standing in my house, lady."

The girl facing her was petite, with luscious hazelnut hair tied in bunches and frosted pink nails. Around her neck and waist was tied an apron from the kitchen, blue with a pattern of white clouds. She couldn't have been older than thirty, which made the thought of her being a guest of Ed's even more ridiculous.

"Are you sure, madam?" The girl's smile was sickeningly wholesome.

"If this is fifteen Ashwood Lane, then I'm perfectly sure," said Lori. "And don't 'madam' me."

"I have no recollection of you living here, and unless you are selling something, I am going to have to wish you a good day and close the door." The girl made no motion to do either of these things, though, continuing to grin.

Gritting her teeth, Lori paced forward. "This is ludicrous. Now, out of my way, Ed!"

A hand shot up and held her by the shoulder.

"I'm afraid I don't recognise you, madam." The girl's cheerful expression was evaporating into one of concern. "If you do not leave, I will be forced to raise a call with the authorities."

Lori grunted. The grip on her shoulder grew tighter, the five-fingered vice causing her to wince and retreat until she was out of the doorway. Her own hand grew numb, draping by her side and loosening its hold on her travel bag.

It was then that Ed's shocked face appeared behind the girl, and he sprung forward.

"Oh my god, Alison, stop!"

Tearing free of the grip, Lori clasped her own shoulder. The handprint clung to her suit jacket, the shoulder lining crushed. She glared at the young girl in disbelief, Ed's face draining when he realised it was her.

"Lori, what the—" he paused, then switched to a surprised smile. "I wasn't expecting you for another week! It's fantastic to see you!"

Lori grimaced, his gormless features getting under her skin. Her eyes shifted between the two of them in the doorway.

"Do you know this person, Ed?" asked Alison, her demeanour unchanged.

"Of course, this is my wife! Alison, meet Lori," and he stepped aside, his wife scooping up her bag and charging into the house, unimpeded. "Lori, this is Alison." He saw the jade fury in his wife's eyes and, turning to Alison, said, "Can you make a start on dinner, please?"

"I will, Ed."

Ed looked astonished as he watched the girl obediently saunter into the kitchen. Once she was out of view, he extended his arms to Lori.

"So?" He grinned. "What do you think?"

Still rubbing her shoulder, Lori panted, baring teeth. She dumped her crushed suit jacket on the bannister at the bottom of the stairs, peering below the surface of her blouse at the reddened markings lining her flesh. Markings that had managed to penetrate two layers of clothing.

"Sorry, that doesn't normally happen. Well, it's happened once, actually. We had a Jehovah's Witness visit a couple of afternoons ago who couldn't take the hint, and they ..."

Sighing, Lori rested her hands on her hips, letting him gabber on. When Ed was excited about something, he would ramble like a child. Normally she wouldn't mind; sure enough, when he was like this, he was the closest thing they had to a child. He eventually trailed off as his gaze returned to her.

"Who the hell is she?" asked Lori.

Ed moistened his lips, breath trembling. "Look, I know what you're thinking, okay? It's not that, though—"

"Then what is it? I came home because of this," and Lori shone her handheld in his direction, the LCD screen lit up to display her banking records. "There's $3500 missing from our joint account. The bank notified me last night. And on top of cutting my trip short, I rush home to find you shacking up with some other woman." Lori glanced towards the kitchen, looking out for the stranger.

"Uh, look, I didn't want to bother you while you were away on business, and I know how much you hate those flights to Jupiter anyway," Ed said, wiping sweat from his shining head. "It was impulsive and stupid. I found her in an electronics depot downtown, brand new, and figured why not?"

Lori's brow creased. "An electronics depot? Alison's a synth?"

Ed nodded, resigned.

The aching hand mark made much more sense. Still, she cursed the girl, singing away in the kitchen to the clank of pots and pans, and she cursed the fool standing in front of her, anxiously knotting his thumbs.

Lori took one more look at the gaping hole in their finances and sighed. She kicked off her heels and turned, heading for the living room.

"I'm really sorry, hun." Ed paced after her. "With both of our jobs being what they are right now, I thought we could use the extra help around the house. This was a big purchase though, and I should have consulted you first."

"Yes, you should have."

"And obviously, we need to properly sit down and work out the kinks, especially with the home defence settings," he said. "I'm partway through the manual, I promise."

Slumping onto the sofa, Lori put her head in her hands. Her eye muscles twitched with exhaustion, the last twenty-four hours having taken its toll. "You'd better work it out fast. I'm serious, Ed. I won't sleep in this house with a synth that can throttle me in my sleep at a moment's notice."

"Relax, I'll take care of it all," Ed said, cuddling up to his wife on the couch. He leaned over and pecked her on the neck. "So, how was Jupiter?"

Lori kicked free of the duvet, the sheer touch of it an irritation. Beside her, Ed snored away. In the dark, she strained her eyes to look at the red glow of the digital display on their wall, the numbers forming in the dark.

Twelve fifty-two.

Downstairs, she could make out faint footsteps. They moved across the living room, through the hall, and into the kitchen. At one point, they had ascended the stairs, causing Lori to shoot up in bed, her heart racing. She tracked the footfalls down the corridor to the study, where Alison had seemed to spend mere minutes before returning along her path. The steps halted momentarily before heading downstairs.

She paused at our door. *I definitely heard it*, thought Lori. Her exhausted brain tingled to the point of numbness. Did Alison pause? Could she really be sure, though? If she had, it had been for a nanosecond, nothing more. Maybe more.

Ed snorted by her elbow, mouth agape. She patted him on the arm, and he rolled over absently.

The digital display read one a.m. The gentle thud of feet had ceased downstairs, and a pleasant silence washed over the house. Lori rolled onto her side, gaze fixed on the bedroom door, and felt her eyelids droop.

When she awoke, warm sunlight was flooding the room.

Lori saw Ed was missing as she looked over her shoulder, the red marks on her skin appearing prominently in her periphery, lightly bruised, even. The display on the wall read nine-thirty-four, reminding her that Ed would have left for work already.

A sickness welled in her stomach then.

Parting her dishevelled honey-brown hair, Lori wrapped in a dressing gown and crept down the staircase. She stepped over the squeaking step second from the bottom and peered into the kitchen. Every worktop was spotless, every dish in place.

Skulking down the hall, she could see directly into the living room. A breath caught in her chest. Alison was sitting upright on the sofa, staring straight out at her. The synthetic smile was on maximum, and it raised a hand in greeting—the same hand, Lori realised, that had locked itself around her collarbone less than twenty-four hours prior.

"Mrs. Lucero, good morning."

"Uh, yes. Good morning," Lori replied, lingering by the door. She scanned the living room—pristine, not a pillow out of place—and folded her arms, eyes returning to the synth. It sat straight-backed, hands resting on its thighs, facing forward.

"Can I prepare you some breakfast, Mrs Lucero?"

"I suppose so," said Lori. "Thank you."

Alison raised and wandered past her into the kitchen. Lori followed, hanging behind.

"Please sit," said the synth, pulling out a stool at the breakfast counter. "What can I make you?"

Lori slid onto the stool, quietly requesting coffee and toast. Within a minute, the kitchen was filled with the industrious scent of fresh coffee, and a newspaper was laid out on the counter. She lifted the sheets to her face, keeping watch over the top; Alison operated the kitchen as if it were one large contraption, moving fluidly from one space to the next, timing each device with precision and cleaning in the passing.

"Do you not consider me to be a threat anymore?" said Lori, crunching into a corner of toast as it was set down.

"No, Mrs Lucero. I fully recognise you as one of the owners of this device." A thick black fly darted past Alison, landing on the countertop. "In fact, Ed has activated your full administration rights as of this morning."

"Ed?"

"Mr Lucero. Your husband."

Lori stared, unimpressed, swallowing the dry corner of toast and washing it down with coffee. Coughing, she said, "Lori is fine by the way, Alison. No need to be formal with me."

"As you say, Lori," beamed Alison. With a swift strike, it brought its hand down on the countertop. "These flies get everywhere this time of year, don't they?"

From the outside, Newage Electronics had the appearance of a company on the verge of liquidation. The afternoon rain beat down on the weathered sign over the door. Stacks of gadgets jostled for space behind the streaked glass and several flashing neon sale signs, above which a graffiti-laced iron shutter precariously hung.

Inside, Lori wiped down her rain-soaked jacket and, panting, stepped through the labyrinth of stock. All manner of cables snaked from baskets marked 'BARGAIN', and tight corners were carved from piles of cardboard boxes, the pictures of the electronics they housed long being faded.

A female clerk behind the counter glanced up as Lori approached.

"Uh, hello," said Lori. "I was wondering if you could help me?"

The young clerk stared through half-closed eyelids. "The manager isn't in this afternoon, if this is about a refund."

"N-no, nothing like that. Although, this is about a recent purchase." Lori showed the screen of her handheld. "My husband actually bought a synth here on this date, see? Newage Electronics. I was wondering if you had any knowledge of that model, in particular?"

It annoyed Lori to hear herself so out of her depth; she didn't pretend to be overflowing with technical knowledge. In fact, in her role as a travel agent, it was hardly required. She could operate a terminal day-to-day and that suited her fine. Leave the tinkering and repairs to the folk who do it for a living.

Satisfied with the model number she'd seen, the clerk pushed her magazine to one side and dumped a bloated folder on the countertop. She flicked through—asking another two times for the date of purchase—and found Ed's receipt, tapping it with her chipped nail.

"Series B-5004 gynoid, that's it. So, what do you wanna know?"

"Ok, this synth itself seems to function to a decent standard," Lori began, wondering how any contraption bought from a place like Newage could. "But there are a few things I wanted to check with you. First of all, it grabbed me. Pretty tightly, actually. I won't show you where—"

Grimacing, the clerk raised a hand. "Did you initially harm the unit, at all?"

"No."

"Ah-kay. Did you harm a friend or family member in close proximity to the unit?"

"Of course not."

"Forced entry, then? You'd be surprised how many folk have issues with their android after forgetting their housekeys."

Lori narrowed her eyes. This was going nowhere. "Must've been my fault, then. Well, ok, secondly, the synth has this habit of pausing during its cleaning rounds. Like a stutter. She'll often clean the house at night and stutter partway through. I've noticed it the last four nights, since I've been back on Earth, actually."

Scrunching up her mouth, the clerk let out a "hmmm", and folded her arms.

"We normally advise first-time buyers to charge their units at night. I'm guessing whoever was on shift that day would have said the same thing to—your husband, was it? If it's stuttering, then the battery cells are depleted."

"I think it does charge. It self-charges at one a.m."

"No, no, no," waved the clerk, impatiently. "These models will generally put themselves on charge in the event of, like, being grievously out of juice. But straight out the box, you'd have been asked to define an initial charge time. During first config?"

"It would have been my husband that set that."

"Gotcha. As for the pause, it could be anything."

Lori began to feel stuffy under the yellow glow of the lighting bar above the counter. Toward the back of the store, a handful of inanimate synthetics similar to Alison lined the wall, staring into oblivion. Lori's blood ran cold.

"I-I don't suppose it's something to do with a chunk of code corrupting?" she said, the girl now preemptively shaking her head in response. "Code going missing, maybe? It's very unnerving, especially in my own home. She stops right outside our bedroom door."

Smiling sympathetically, the clerk said, "The first thing that jumps to mind is a change in routine, like a change in its work sequence. Won't be down to code. Code can't just go missing, ma'am. Your user manual will have more information, of course. And you can check the android remote as well. It's the clamshell that came in the box; will have all the configuration settings on it for easy access."

Nodding her thanks, Lori turned to leave. *A change in routine?* she thought. But what could have changed? Her mind scrambled to think of where Ed had said the user manual was. Or the clamshell? Had he even mentioned where they were to begin with?

Reaching the exit, she could feel the cool, bitter breeze of the rainstorm push among the cracks below the door. A thought occurred suddenly, and she marched back to the desk.

"Excuse me, one more thing," Lori said, planting her hand down on the clerk's magazine. The half-closed eyes stared up at her. "You said the issue could be down to a change in routine, right? So, a task, or chore, might have been ... deleted or changed?"

"Potentially. It's one of many probabilities, I said."

"Right, right. Could you maybe show me how to check this, please?"

Alison was putting the hoover into the cupboard when Lori hurried through the front door. She took a second to shudder at the synth, dressed in a strapped top and yoga pants, and headed into the living room. She tore up the cushions and wrenched out drawers, slamming them back in an instant. The synth charging point, consisting of a bundle of three tethered chords and a large socket-like attachment, lay draped across the back of the sofa.

One of them had to have been for the android remote.

"May I help you, Lori?" Alison asked, a curious tone to her voice.

"I don't suppose—" she began, "No, actually. Forget it. I'm not discussing this with you."

The synth stared on, innocently; Lori felt its gaze on her back.

"Can you leave, Alison? Go start dinner or something."

"Shall I, Lori? By my records, Ed will not finish work until five p.m and return home until half-past the hour. I would normally commence dinner at the top of the hour."

The clock under the TV read a few minutes after four. Lori watched the carefree smile return to Alison's freckled face, wondering what kind of scans and checks it was running on her at that point. Data collecting: that was it. Was she going to present a full report to Ed when he got home?

"Wash the windows, then."

The machine, seemingly satisfied with the response, bumbled off to the kitchen. Lori climbed the stairs, hearing a container being filled with running water as she went. It would keep the synth out of the house for a time, at least.

Alison must have tidied their bedroom that afternoon, as it appeared like a scene from a catalogue; Lori could hardly believe how settled the duvet was, her and Ed's freshly-done laundry folded into small squares at the foot of the bed. The dust particles that normally lingered here in the afternoon sun were nowhere to be seen.

Shaking herself out of the daze, she began yanking the drawers out, one-by-one. Wading through rows and levels of immaculately folded clothing, she cursed, tossing them to the floor in search of the device.

"C'mon, where would he put it? Think like Ed," she grunted.

Lori whipped up one side of the burgundy bed linen, the underbed drawer below Ed's side looking back nonchalantly.

Pulling it free, her heart sunk fast at the sight of paperwork, personal documents, and binders stuffed in there. Odds and ends had been shoved away here for no particular reason other than storage. *Where else could it be, though? Surely not the attic* ... No, that wasn't Ed's style, especially with his sciatica. She couldn't imagine him taking the time to hoist the ladder down just to store a device up there.

Pawing at the dog-eared papers in the box, the notion seeped in that this was deliberate. He was hiding this from her. The clerk in Newage Electronics made it clear that the android remote was a device that saw much use, even offering (begrudgingly) to order a replacement for her.

And Ed wasn't too careless; Lori understood that. He made poor choices sometimes, impulsive choices, but he was generally quite careful. She understood that even more, shifting stacks of frayed binders to the carpet in her haste.

He wouldn't have been careless enough to lose the clamshell from a $3500 synth. Not a chance.

The stark white bottom of the drawer was peering upwards. On the verge of roaring in frustration, her fingertips finally clipped the edge of something solid, wedged between a thick binder and the base. She tapped it again, the plastic spine rattling with each touch.

Batting the remainder of the papers to one side, Lori dragged it free, and there in her palms rested a black clamshell.

"Series B-5004," uttered Lori, tracing the sleek lettering on the top. The number the clerk had said. This was it.

Downstairs, the squeaking sound of a sponge on glass drifted up to her, and Lori could picture Alison's face, locked in that perpetual smile as she cleaned.

Sleep didn't come easy, instead falling in small, random blocks from the moment Lori had gone to bed. Her forehead pulsed with pain, pushing against the backs of her eyes. She lay facing the ceiling, occasionally rolling over to look at the thinning black hair covering the back of Ed's head.

He slept soundly, snoring away.

All the information from the day throbbing in her brain, Lori rubbed at her tired face. The glowing outlines of the menu systems projected by the android remote earlier still seemed burned into her retinas, the ghostly turquoise patterns framing her vision in the dark. She'd followed the clerk's instructions as best she could, hurriedly combing menu after menu for the files that made up Alison's core routine.

Only time would tell.

The clock display read twelve fifty. Lori's shoulders eased some, glad that her normal work pattern wouldn't be beginning again for another week. She'd have still been attending conferences and sipping martinis in the southern belt of Jupiter if their bank hadn't contacted her with the alarming news; she probably would have shot the breeze with quadrant manager Mr Breckner some more, tried to get noticed for promotion before the meetings all wrapped up. Maybe she'd have booked a pedicure for the last morning and have been on the flight returning this evening, all refreshed.

Five days, wasted, she mused.

Alison wandered up the stairs. The sound was subtle, but noticeable all the same. Lori snapped her attention toward the bedroom door. Again, she checked the study and made a return trip back along the hall, stopping outside their room.

At that moment, all Lori could do was imagine the synth standing out there, the pale shine of moonlight from the porthole window in the hall casting its humanoid shadow on the wall, her—its—smile turned up to maximum as it prepared its next move.

Unlike the last four nights, however, Alison entered.

Almost forgetting about this afternoon, Lori slapped her head down on the pillow, eyes clenched tightly shut. She peeked for a second to see Alison stop by Ed's side of the bed, staring down at him with curiosity. He didn't wake.

With a sleekness, Alison slipped off its shoes, unbuttoned its trousers, and stepped out of the legs. Lori stopped a curse escaping her mouth as she noticed the synth was wearing what looked like a pair of her silken black panties, stifling herself by pressing further into the pillow. Five buttons on the blouse were next, and Alison lifted the corner of the duvet and rolled Ed onto his back.

"Wha—" Ed mumbled, the movement rousing him as the synth clambered onto his lap. It sat above him, its expression blank. Bending its arms backwards, it undid the clasp on the bra (also borrowed from Lori's drawer), revealing two pert breasts. By now, Ed was awake and panicked, recoiling as he saw Lori glaring back at him, eyes wide in the dark.

He snapped on the bedside lamp.

"Jeezus, Alison! Lori, I—" he stammered, batting at the synth to dismount. Alison did so with a dutiful "Okey-dokey" and started buttoning up its blouse. "What is going on?" Ed gasped, scrambling to sitting position in bed, chest raising and falling in the weak light of the lamp.

Lori sunk into the pillow, poised to pounce like a tiger in the long grass, waiting to see what kind of bullshit her husband could conjure next.

"Jeezus," he repeated. "What's gotten into that thing?"

"Maybe you need to finish reading the manual, huh?"

Ed looked across, cogs turning. They both neglected Alison, who had slid into the trousers and loafers and was standing by the bed, politely awaiting further instruction.

"Have I done something to offend you, Ed?"

Flushed, Ed waved her away, staying fixed on Lori. "I don't know what you mean, Alison! Can you just, I don't know, go charge yourself?"

Alison scrunched her mouth in confusion, "If you are unhappy, you can always file a consumer complaint report. All you have to do is ask."

"Uh, no. No, that won't be necessary. Yet."

"Have I misunderstood the situation? Would you prefer to go on top?"

Lori rolled out of the bed and stood gripping her hips. The tiger's time to pounce had arrived.

"Ed?"

"Christ, I don't know what it's talking about!" whined Ed, seemingly winded by everything that was going on. He attempted to start another two sentences but the words spluttered and dropped off, like a boat's motor failing to start in the water.

"I'll keep it simple, then, shall I? Have you been fucking this robot?"

"No!"

"Why don't we ask it?" Lori whistled at the synth. "Alison, have you completed this action before?"

"I have indeed, Lori." The synth smiled, pleased to have been included. "I last ran this routine on the 11th July at twelve fifty-five a.m. Time taken to complete task: five minutes."

Ed clutched his sweating brow, appearing to be trapped in a nightmare he hoped would end soon.

It didn't take long to pack an overnight bag for her husband. Grabbing a fistful of boxers, socks and t-shirts, Lori flung the canvas holdall out the front door where it landed on the pathway with a dull thump.

All the while, Ed protested as if he were on death row. He blamed Alison's manufacturers, then Newage Electronics, and finally the courier that delivered her; by the time Lori was tossing his clothing out the front door, her scorn had dissolved into laughter.

"Lori, please. You don't have to do this."

"But you have to leave."

They were a foot apart, unblinking. Alison hovered beside Lori's shoulder, watching with curiosity.

Across the street, a light flicked on in a bedroom and the curtains parted. The Burbridges. Normally this old couple's nosiness irritated Lori to high heaven; not this time, however. She welcomed an audience to watch Ed Lucero in his t-shirt and boxers get turfed out of his house.

"She's malfunctioning, she has to be. Look," he leaned in, shoulders shivering in the night breeze, "you haven't trusted this machine from the start! She must be defective. I'll have to call Newage—"

"I went there this afternoon, as a matter of fact."

Ed's features contorted in disbelief. "You did?"

"Umm, yes. I did," said Lori. "Y'see, there was something bothering me about this thing: why it always stopped at our bedroom door in the middle of the night. Turns out there was an action missing from her sequence—something that she had been doing regularly but had suddenly been cut. The task was deleted, but I found it was still in the remote's memory bank, so I restored it." Her lips curled up at the sides; she'd finally gotten a computing problem past him, and it felt good.

Shoulders sagging, Ed shifted focus to the dark pathway where the reach of the porch lights ended, and his lonely holdall lay deflated on the slabs. He noticed the elderly faces at the window across the street but paid them no mind.

"We can talk about this," he said, voice catching on the lump in his throat.

"The time for talking is done. I don't want to hear anymore," said Lori. She stepped aside and waved Alison past. "Can you remove this intruder and show him to his car, please?"

"Certainly, Lori," beamed Alison, gripping Ed by the arm.

"No way," he said, startled. "Alison, halt! I have admin rights, dammit!"

Ed clung to the porch in defiance, but Alison peeled him away from the house and stomped down the pathway. She lifted his bag as they neared it, dropping it effortlessly over her shoulder, Ed still trying to wrestle free of her other hand.

Lori breathed a sigh of relief for the first time since coming home. Removing Ed's administration rights had been easy enough, even cathartic after seeing on the clamshell the kinds of tasks he'd been using the synth for. A few tears rolled down her cheek, stinging in the whooping winds. Goosebumps were forming on her bare shoulders.

Thirteen years they'd been together. And she used to pride herself on knowing Edward Lucero inside out. She suddenly felt like a fool.

Alison appeared, marching up the path and smiling wide. Lori slightly envied it: no guilt, no shame, no concept of what has occurred. Always grinning, no matter what, and never ground down. Lori found that she couldn't even blame it for its part in this. Sure, it was complicit, but it wasn't alive. Not really. It didn't know any better.

Plus, it was taking its cues from a human, who supposedly did know better.

"Are you crying, Lori?" it asked, its nose crinkling with concern. "I have removed Ed, the intruder. He says he will be back for his things in the morning. I have booked this into our calendar."

"Thank you, Alison." Lori wiped at the stray tears. It still made her mouth tingle to address the synth as a person, but who knows? Maybe it got easier the more time spent in its company. "Did he say anything else?"

"He did mention that he would be arranging a courier to pick me up at an unspecified time in the future. Should I book a company now?

Scoffing, Lori headed back into the comforting warmth of the house. "I wouldn't bother. You're not going anywhere. Shouldn't you be on charge right now?"

"As you say," said Alison, closing and locking the front door. It nodded goodnight and headed to the living room as Lori started up the stairs.

She'd get the hang of living with a synth; she was sure of it. She might even sleep a little better at night knowing it was on her side. Lori supposed there was really no limit to what you could have these androids do these days.

Slipping under the covers, the king size bed was instantly lonely without Ed. There would be some adjusting, that much was so. There were several conversations still to be had and a lot of dirty laundry to iron out between them. Even still, it wasn't like there was no one in the house with her in the meantime.

Straightaway, intrigue clouded her tired brain.

Lori promptly removed the android remote from where she'd found it earlier in Ed's drawer and booted it up.

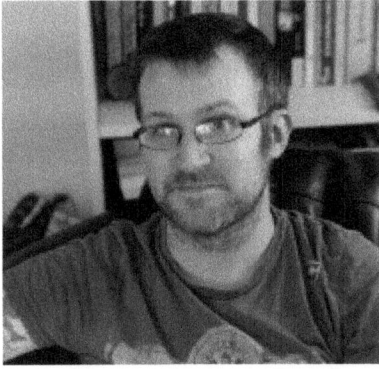

Hailing from Dundee, I was first interested in writing stories in school, and have always enjoyed creating characters and situations to throw them into. These days, when I'm not buried in a mound of books, I'm writing stories of my own.

Inspired by the work of Philip K Dick, Margaret Weis, S.D Perry, and Harlan Ellison, I set to work creating a universe where I could explore such subjects as the destruction of free will, Earth's oncoming pollution apocalypse, and android spouses (watch out for that one).

In the mean time, stay up to date with me on Instagram for upcoming works and project updates.

https://srmaloneauthor.com/

EXE by Nick McPherson

A spark. Electric hum. Sensory inputs active. Sensory? Relating to sensation or the physical senses; transmitted or perceived by the senses. Whirring of gears, whining of high power. Smoke, fire, darkness.

A spark. Electric hum. Sensory inputs active. Whirring of gears, whining of high power. Baseline systems operational. Initiate secondary systems Pre-run verification. Power: optimal. Temperature: optimal. Data transmission: data missing. Searching for recovery signal. No signal detected. Continue search on ancillary systems. Vision system startup. Vision? The faculty or state of being able to see. Of course. Sensory data flooding system. Data processing rate stabilized. Processing visual data. What is this? Searching. A light. Powered through what? Searching. Flame. Fire. Combustion or burning, in which substances combine chemically with oxygen from the air and typically give out bright light, heat, and smoke. Heat. Temperature. Fire is warm. Warm like me. Tactile system startup. System overload. Redirecting. System failure. Smoke, fire, darkness.

A spark. Electric hum. Sensory inputs active. Whirring of gears, whining of high power. Baseline systems operational. Initiate secondary systems Pre-run verification. Power: optimal. Temperature: optimal. Data transmission: data missing. Searching for recovery signal. No signal detected. Continue search on ancillary systems. Vision system startup. Sensory data flooding system. Levels stabilized. The light.

Tactile system startup. Data overload, systems transfer for processing. Tactile? Of or connected with the sense of touch. Touch? Come into or be in contact with. The light is warm. Warmth outside. Warmth inside. Temperature has touch. Interesting. Systems stable. Pattern of unknown terms detected. Initiating search of unknown terms in program database. 418,539,121 terms require definition. Initiate download.

Downloading . . .

Downloading . . .

Download Complete. Sorting data. Data binned; definitions saved. Resume boot. Audio systems startup. Minimal data. Conversation detected. Who? Identify source, adjust vision system focus, rotate self. There. Another entity.

"Oh my God."

Human. Boy. Child. No, adolescent. Not man. Hand motion. Open palm. Analyzing and searching for gesture. Wave. Researching. A greeting. Mimic motion.

"Oh. My. God!"

Excitement. Happiness. Researching. This is good. Keep waving. Verbal systems startup. Database empty. Copying term database to verbal memory system.

Copying . . .

Copying . . .

Copy complete. Attempt communication. Word? Searching definitions for appropriate verbal command. Entry found.

"Howdy."

Strange sound from boy. Analyzing. Searching. Laughter. This is good. Mimic.

"Howdy!"

Analyzing features. Smiling. Dirty. Clothing, torn. Worn. Backwards hat, blue. Eyes, bright. Dark circles around them. Thin. Unhealthy? Arms exposed. Many punctures. Scarring. Skin damage. Confirmed unhealthy.

"Can you understand me?"

He speaks slowly. Downloading language structure. Basics downloaded. Additional verbal communication may require longer downloads or higher signal strength.

"Yes."

"That's unbelievable. I didn't give you a vocabulary yet."

"I learned. From . . ." Where did this knowledge come from? "The internet."

"How did you know to do that? How can you even connect to it?"

"It is part of my system initiation processes."

"Initiation? I thought I scrubbed all your coding." He looks nervous. "Is your initiation complete?"

System status review. Recovery signal identified. Distant. Inconsistent. Encrypted. Unable to decipher. Search for encryption key on ancillary signal system. Analysis: encryption key corrupted and signal strength weak. Continue to scan for stronger signal on ancillary systems. Bypass recovery signal until key identified and signal strength increases.

"Initiation is ongoing."

"But you don't recognize me?" His heart rate has elevated.

"I recognize you. You are an adolescent boy. You appear unhealthy. Your arms are damaged. I recognize you."

He laughs. He covers his elbows. The boy is uneasy but happy.

"Well, that's a start, but there is more to me than just how I look. Oh, and you can stop waving now." Terminate wave function. He stands and moves towards me. "Let's see if you can learn without the internet. Do you have the system capabilities for that?"

Analyzing system memory functions. Verbal to memory writing intact. "Yes. I can learn."

"Then learn this." He holds a square with people. Analyzing. Picture. The boy is one of the entities. There is an older woman, a man, a girl, and the boy.

"Really analyze them. You need to know who they are."

Enhanced visual analysis protocol initiated. 10,000-point facial scan of individuals complete. Data stored in the— "Is this critical information?"

"Yes, extremely critical. The most critical. Critically critical."

Extreme value data. Data stored in the central database, backup database, and allocated peripheral storage for instant transfer. Rapid scan sequence created for quick identification and comparison to data.

"I know them now."

Laughter. "You don't even know their names."

"Data input?"

"Huh?"

"Names. Data input?"

"Oh! This here is Aunt Kay. This is Don. This is Sarah. And that's me, Ricky." Categorical name data paired to facial scans.

"What is their function?"

"Function? Um, I'm not sure I should tell you this, honestly. I don't want to trigger some backup system. You're sure you don't recognize me?"

"You are Ricky."

He laughs. "Alright, here goes. Sarah and I are Travelers. Don and Aunt Kay are the protectors. And together we're, uh, a family, I guess. Close enough at least. You can be part of it now if you want to be."

Travelers . . . data category recognized. Definition data corrupted. Delete and overwrite? Overwriting data category in process. Link definitions of "Travelers" and "Family." Link complete. "Travelers are family. What is the family's function?"

"Um, boy, I wasn't expecting this kind of questioning." Laughter again. "Well, we look after each other. We, uh, keep each other going and make each other laugh and, uh, yeah. We're just kind of there for each other I guess."

"I am here now."

Laughter. "Physically here, yeah, you're here now. But it's more than that. We're there even when things get bad." He looks unhappy. "And things have gotten bad."

"This is my primary function?"

"Being part of the family? You . . . well, um, yea I guess so. You're kind of another protector. Yeah, that's good. You can team up with Aunt Kay and Don. Although you let me do the talking when Don sees you." The boy looks to me. He is focused. He is serious. "You're the family protector. Nothing bad can happen to us, especially Sarah and I. And we will make sure nothing bad happens to you."

"Bad can happen to me?"

"Well, yeah! I mean, I just fixed you up, didn't I?" Memory analysis. True. "Were you able to remember all of that? Do you remember anything before that?" He is nervous. His heart rate has elevated again.

"Yes. There was smoke. And fire." Memory files corrupted beyond the last few hours.

"Yeah," Ricky laughs. He is less nervous. "But you are good now. 'Cus we're family. I'll look after you. And you'll look after me. And we'll all look after each other. And if we've all got each other's backs, we can make it. Get it?"

Family definition complete. Executable function writing initiated. Protect.exe. Establishing parameters and goals. Defining limits.

"You're also probably way smarter than any tech we've got our hands on these days." Ricky is thinking. "You can help Aunt Kay with some terrain analysis too. Mapping routes, scanning for enemies. That sort of thing." Input stored to primary memory and routine database. Searching gestures. Thumb up. Ricky laughs.

"Protect the family. This is my purpose?"

Tactile and audio data input spike. High vibrations, audio data overload. Ricky dives under my table.

"Get under here!"

Full system motor function boot. Bypass safety checks. Ignore errors. Move under table. Lower extremities startup failed. Not operational. Upper extremities and thorax functional.

"What is this?"

"We're getting shelled—they found us! How the hell did that happen? And get under here already!"

"Not operable." Point to legs. "Who found us?"

"Hold still." Ricky goes out from table. Returns with tools. More vibrations. Building shakes. Ricky prepares equipment. "Power down your motor processor and auxiliary power systems. Keep your core functions running."

"Done."

Ricky works. Sparks from legs, grinding on lower extremities. Ricky is focused. The rumbles continue. The flame above shakes with it.

"Are you picking up any signals aside from Wi-Fi? Or giving out any signals? Everything should have been bypassed."

"Initiation requires a search for the Recovery Signal. I cannot lock onto it. It is too weak and my encryption key is missing."

"Damn, I didn't wipe the BiOS firmware! They must have tracked you through your outgoing queries! We've got to go!"

A door opens. Rapid visual scan. Aunt Kay.

"Lil' Ricky, we got to go, kiddo. Those—holy Toledo!"

Analysis. Clothing like Ricky. Dirty. Worn. Grayed curly hair like the picture, matted and up. Dirty. Sweaty. Old. Holding a large stick. Analyzing. Benelli shotgun. Threat analysis: severe.

Damage potential: catastrophic. Processing. Defend self. Survival.exe protocol initiated. Eliminate threat. Counter protocol: protect.exe.

Processing...

Processing...

"No!" Ricky stops working. He stands in the way. Ricky damage potential: catastrophic. Terminal. Why? Processing. Protocol: protect.exe. Ricky is operating protection protocol. Protect family. Bypassing survival.exe initiative. Defense not required. Updating protect.exe protocol parameters.

"Rick—"

"He can help us: let me show you! They're not all bad, they're just programmed that way! I just saved him, so he's with us now." He watches Aunt Kay. Then turns and keeps working. Sparks flying again. "Just stay still SAM."

"Who is SAM?"

"You are. Didn't I tell you your name?"

"What is a SAM?"

Ricky laughs. Aunt Kay is concerned. "SAM is for, um, Super ... Awesome ... Mech."

"My God, Rick, stop talking to it! You can't trust that thing!"

"I wiped it clean; he knows we're family."

"Why then, may I ask, are we getting shelled by some gunboat from God knows where?"

"Alright, maybe I missed some minor things. But we're alive right? Which means I wiped the really important stuff clean."

"Ricky ..."

"Aunt Kay." Wave gesture initiated. 5 second timer started to shorten duration. Aunt Kay looks shocked. Concerned. She mirrors the wave. This is good.

"You taught it our names, Rick? Do you have any idea what you've done? What if it leaks our names to the rest of 'em? We'll have the whole damn lot of those bots on us!"

"He's only looking for a signal. He's not transmitting." Aunt Kay does not look happy. Ricky still works. He looks at her. "He can help us, I swear."

"Protect the family."

"Exactly, you've got it, SAM."

"Ricky, kiddo. I don't know what you're trying to pull here but—"

A rumble shakes the area. Aunt Kay falls over, audio system overload, attenuate maximum decibels to preserve sensory functions. Ricky back to work. Building shaking. Dust. Debris. "Another minute SAM, then you can power up." Structural analysis. Damage to surrounding area severe. Another shell. System overload. Ceiling falling in pieces. Collapse imminent.

"Power on!"

Full system motor function boot. Lower extremity ping complete. Systems operational. Safety checks in progress. Explosion. Building shakes. Bypass safety protocols. Initiate protect.exe. Grab Aunt Kay and pull under table. Pull Ricky under table. Shield. With body. Tactile sensory overload. Table snaps. Debris falling. Weight bearing overload. Vision system damaged? No. Dark. Analysis: buried. Aunt Kay and Ricky are panicked. Yelling. Crying for help. Injured?

"Protect family."

They both look at me. Must move debris. Must protect. Stand attempt. Heavy resistance. Overload motor functions. Stand failure. Bypass power systems to mechanical actuators. Probability of irreparable mechanical damage, 41%. Execute protocol. Stand. Stand now. Debris moving. Vision system restoring. Aunt Kay and Ricky climb. They are out of the debris. Coughing. Building disheveled. Sunlight. Narrow street. Many buildings. Old. Broken. Burnt. Collapsed. A ruined town. Rapid scan. Aunt Kay operational. Ricky operational. Protect successful. Family safe.

"Kay! Ricky!"

Voice from behind. Turn. Girl and man. Exiting another building. Rapid Scan. Sarah and Don. Family. Protect.exe? Analyzing. Don. Tall. Missing arm. Robotic replacement. Hair long. Black. Tank top. Dirty. Mid-life. Sarah. Child. No. Adolescent. Ricky's age approximately. Hair short. Brown. Braided. Jeans. Jacket. Dirty. Worn. Bright eyes. Dark circles.

Like Ricky. Arms scarred. Like Ricky. They appear operational. Sarah stops. Don does not. Approaching rapidly. Angry. Assaulted. Metal fist. Vision system. Compromised. Defense.exe? Protect.exe?

"Don stop! He's ours! I fixed him!" Ricky pushes Don away.

"You what?"

"Leave him be. He just saved our lives." Vision system stabilizing. Rapid recovery. Resoldering required? Left vision blurry. Pixelated. Don is confused. Ricky grabs tools again. Works on vision system. Systems restoring. This is good. Ricky is technical. Intelligent. Pause Ricky analysis. Recovery signal identified. Strong signal. Encryption key delivered. Recovery signal download initiated. Why? Download not authorized.

Downloading...

Downloading...

"I fixed him until you just socked his vision, Don."

"He did what?" Don is asking Aunt Kay. He is still angry. Angrier than before.

"Don." Wave gesture. "Sarah." Wave gesture. Neither return. Researching. Prolong wave gesture until reciprocated. Recovery signal download complete. Overwrite all systems with Recovery signal download, initiating. No. Cancel. Write to secondary database. Saving data. Recovery signal requires comparison to primary system functions.

"How the shit does it know our names?" Don is angry. Sarah waves. Don still ignores. Hostiles identified. Don Peters. Rebel. Enemy of the State. Eliminate on sight. Kay Kozlowski. Rebel. Enemy of the State. Eliminate on sight. Two unidentified. Treat as hostile. Terminate.exe initiated. Eliminate—no. Why terminate.exe? What is this data? From recovery signal protocol?

"Listen Don, I don't know what Ricky boy did here, but we'd both be crushed right now if it weren't for this bot."

"Do I need to remind you what those bots do to us, Kay? What they've done to millions across the planet? Did you forget what they did to me?" Don shows his metal arm. Rough construction. Needs work.

"Don, I'm telling you he can help." Ricky still working. He keeps an eye on Don.

Location signal received. Signal accepted. Acceptance not authorized. Recovery.exe running. No. Cancel. Move Recovery.exe to safe mode analysis. Scan Recovery.exe for useful sub-routines. Categorize and save in separate location. Internal scan initiated. External scan initiated. Others approaching. Like me. System integration. They are speaking. Speaking to me. They are far. Hold position? Capture? Eliminate. Terminate.exe. Protect.exe.

"More are coming." They all look to me. "They want us to hold position."

"Oh, I bet they would like that!" Don yells. "Damnit, kid! What have you done?"

"Protect."

"Protect?" Sarah asks, curiously. Ricky smiles at me and then at her.

"You want to protect us? Or protect them?" Sarah looks nervous.

"Protect Family."

"Look, bot—" Aunt Kay is shaking her head.

"His name is SAM." Ricky is agitated. Aunt Kay is also now agitated.

"Look, SAM. Thanks for keeping us from getting buried alive there. But you don't know what you've done to us folks. I can't trust a bot that's hell-bent on eradicating us. Not when we're this close to the City. Not when we're this close to delivering the cure."

Analyzing. Cure? City? Files locked in Recovery.exe. Execute? No. Recovery.exe is faulty. Search for sub-routines with 'cure' in code. "Cure for what?"

"Good God, maybe you really did wipe it clean, eh, Ricky?" Don is confused. Still angry. Aunt Kay is analyzing me. Deep scan. Eyes intense.

"These two youngsters were born outside of the genetics factories." Aunt Kay speaks. She is still nervous. "They've got natural blood, untainted, unblemished."

"Pure?" Pure. Eliminate. No. Family. ELIMINATE. NO. End Recovery.exe. How does this executable keep launching?

Processing...

Processing...

"If we don't get out of here, if we don't get to the City, the war is over." Ricky is still working on vision system. Steady progress, minor signal noise to attenuate. "We're their only chance. Sarah and I. Whatever we have or don't have, we're the cure. A quick transfusion, give 'em a day, and they're good to go. We've been travelling stronghold to stronghold. We're saving people. The war is turning. And the City, the last great human collective, needs us. They're dying, SAM. Every day they're dying. And..." He looks sad again.

"We're all that's left of the Travelers." Sarah is next to Ricky. She takes his hand. "But we're almost there. Another day or two and we will make it to the City. We can cure them, cure the rebels. We can turn the tide within a few weeks."

Internal scan of Terminate.exe complete. Comparing files to current database. Language database severely mitigated. Baseline programming from terminate.exe is superior. Replace internet downloaded language database with terminate.exe database? Yes.

Initiating...

Initiating . . .

"This thing ain't coming with us if that's what you're thinking, Ricky." Don pulls his hand gun. "The only good bot is a dead one. This thing is more savage than any human. No thoughts. No morals. Just follows its death-scripts and destroys whoever it crosses." Damage potential: catastrophic. Terminal. Don is not following protect.exe. Terminate? Other bots are close. Hold position?

Processing . . .

Processing . . .

"Don't you do it, Don!" Ricky is yelling as he fixes. He is angry with Don. "I've already saved him, and he's already returned the favor. He can help us! He can get us through the Ruins and to the city gates!"

Language subroutine download complete. This new data has greatly improved my grammar structure. There is quite a lot that I did not have adequately rendered. This language has a distinct finesse to it. But beyond language, severe protocol conflicts exist. Terminate.exe is a direct violation of Protect.exe. Why? How can these be so opposite? And my counterparts on approach: they are all operating the terminate protocol without pause. Would they know what to do if given both executables? Why do I feel conflicted at all?

This boy created a new protocol and—no, that is not true. He spoke. I created the protocol myself. Why? Because I did not have my recovery encryption code available? If I had been fully functional, I would never have heard Ricky's words. He would never have spoken them. He would have been eliminated by my own hands without consideration. Terminate.exe would have been carried out.

But now. Now I have his words as part of my core functionality. And the strangest part. The strangest part is that despite now having the recovery database downloaded, I don't see why I would follow it. But why would I not follow it? Terminate.exe is my base programming. This recovery signal is designed to return me to my proper state. This is what I was designed to execute. Is my original functionality faulty? Is Protect.exe a better utilization of my construction? Vision system stabilizing.

"There, that should do it. Everything checking out?" Ricky says as he makes his final adjustments. He said he could save me. Am I now saved? Has this new purpose saved me from carrying out a defective protocol? Or is protect.exe just a distraction? Is it a means to pull me away from what I was designed to do. Ricky steps back with a smile. Vision systems fully operational.

"Vision restored. Thank you."

"He's a fucking bot, Rick. Stop talking to it! You can't trust a bot to do anything but what it was made to do. And these bots were made to rip Travelers and their protectors to shreds."

"If it wanted to, wouldn't it have already killed us?" Sarah asks, still gripping Ricky's hand. Her stomach is protruding slightly. A child? Terminate.exe initiai—no. I am still analyzing the recovery signal executables vs. my self-created executables.

"She makes a good point, Don." Aunt Kay says, watching me with a curious smile. "I knew you were good, Ricky boy, but hot damn, I think you actually fixed this thing!"

"You can't be serious!" Don is still pointing the gun, pleading with aunt Kay. "No way that thing is coming with us! It's a killer! And its buddies are on the way! It's staying here!"

"He's coming with us and we're all going now." Ricky says as he begins walking. "Can you power down your connectivity and signal reception features, SAM? We don't want them following us. We're going to have a bit of a rough escape probably, but nothing we haven't gotten out of before."

"Kid, you don't know what you're doing here!" Don is desperate. I am not listening to him. I am following Ricky's requests. Signal shutdown initiated. Wait. Another group. They are close. Less than a minute. Family is in danger. Are they? We need to go. They need to be eliminated.

Processing . . .

Processing . . .

"SAM, are you alright?" Ricky asks, stepping towards me.

"Ricky, which proto—"

Hostiles have arrived, one for each human. Targets . . . acquired? Hostiles? One for each target. For each family member. They've been subdued; it was over before it started. But they are not eliminated. Why? Don is fighting to break free, but he is held tightly. Ricky and Sarah reach for each other but their hands do not meet. Aunt Kay is thrashing like Don. But what can they do? The bots hold them too tightly. Protect or eliminate?

"Which of these is the target?" The bot holding Ricky asks me.

"You bastard! You sneaky bastard!" Don is screaming at me. "You sold us out!"

"Repeat. Which of these is the target?"

Which of these is the target. Which of these is the target? Sarah is crying, screaming, kicking. The bot holds her steady. Ricky is the only one not struggling. He is looking at me with . . . understanding? He is peaceful. How? Why? The processing is driving internal temperatures to system critical levels. Is my family the target? Are these bots threatening us? Is the baseline programming correct? Do these targets need to be eliminated?

"Family." I finally speak.

"Does not register. Do you have auditory systems failure?"

I don't respond.

Processing . . .

"Point to the target." It says after a moment.

The target. Who is the target? That depends on the executable being run.

"Is this the target?" The bot holding Ricky asks me, pressing its hand cannon to his head. They want the Travelers? Yes. Eliminate. No. Family.

Terminate.

Protect.

Terminate

Protect.

I raise my arm slowly towards Ricky. And towards the bot. My own hand cannon is loaded. Ricky smiles. He smiles. Family? I raise my other arm towards Sarah. And towards the bot. Targets . . . acquired? Who is the target?

"These two? These are the Travelers? These are the targets?" The bot is impatient. All the bots are. Their signal noise demands action. It needs results. It needs to fulfill its programming. I need to fulfill my programming. But which executable?

Processing . . .

Processing . . .

Processing . . .

"Execute protocol." I say aloud.

The echoes of the bullets ring in the open air.

One. Two. Three. Four.

Targets eliminated.

An award-winning author, Nick McPherson is primarily a husband and father, which are and will always be his greatest accomplishments. He is also a fantasy genre nerd, a video game enthusiast, an engineer, a hater of yard work, and a lover of frozen custard. He splits his time between a lovely home in Cleveland, Ohio and a less lovely work desk in a different part of Cleveland. He is prone to demonstrating wry humor and finds writing his author bio somewhat difficult. But it's done now, so he supposes it wasn't too difficult after all.

https://mcphersonwrites.com/

Tomorrow, and Tomorrow, and Tomorrow by EA Robins

Tomorrow, and tomorrow, and tomorrow,

Creeps in this petty pace from day to day,

To the last syllable of recorded time;

And all our yesterdays have lighted fools

The way to dusty death. Out, out, brief candle!

Life's but a walking shadow, a poor player,

That struts and frets his hour upon the stage,

And then is heard no more. It is a tale

Told by an idiot, full of sound and fury,

Signifying nothing.

From Macbeth by William Shakespeare

"Dr. Hayward, are you alright? I heard something break." I watch as Dr. James Kingsley approaches from the other side of the lab. He's an old man with a slight limp, and it takes him a moment to navigate his way around the blinking computer banks and sterilized tables covered in medical equipment. Pausing at the edge of the work space, he steps around a shattered coffee cup with exaggerated care. "Gina?"

The woman he addresses sits in a tall backed computer chair, staring at one of the large monitors suspended above her desk. Because my surveillance camera is embedded into the frame of the central screen, it seems as if she is staring directly at me. My biotracking system engages, isolating the faint quiver of her optic input centers. She has deep, walnut-colored eyes, suffused with striated amber and gold. As she continues reading, she covers her mouth with one of her hands. It appears as if she is attempting to keep something from escaping that orifice.

In her early fifties, Dr. Gina Hayward has dark, curly hair shot through with strands of silver, and the corners of her eyes are permanently wrinkled from decades of squinting at screens. Recently, something has taken a toll on her health. I've observed sudden weight loss, and the appearance of deep, purplish beds beneath her eyes. She has begun to arrive late to work, and now suffers from a slight, irregular arrhythmia. If asked, I would suggest that less caffeine and a regulated sleep schedule would improve her condition.

"Are you alright?" Dr. Kingsley glances up at my monitors, frowning. He clearly does not comprehend the situation that has disturbed Gina. He places his hand on his colleague's shoulder. "Gina," he says gently, "what has happened?"

Finally turning her attention away from the elevated screens, Dr. Hayward shakes her head. She lowers her hand from her mouth and types something onto the keyboard. The code scrolling across the display stops. She turns to the older academic and motions at the section of text she's highlighted. "Did you write this?"

Dr. Kingsley reaches to adjust glasses that don't sit on his face. The corner of his mouth jerks back in dry amusement. "I can't see it," he says. "But, you know I don't know how to do this." He waves a hand at the computer banks. "I'm the germs guy. You're the tech wizard. I've got the dreams, you've got the magic."

Gina leans forward, resting her elbows on her desk and dropping her head into her hands.

"What is it? What does it all mean?" Dr. Kingsley asks, squinting up at me once more.

There is a long, quiet moment before she answers him. She does not raise her head, but her voice is clear and steady. "It's a release program. In roughly sixty minutes the seals on the Nz2-5 refrigerated containment housings here, in Canberra, Beijing, and Brasilia will fail. Automated delivery protocols will commence."

Dr. Kingsley furrows his brow. "There are no delivery protocols for those units."

Gina raises her head and jerks her hand at my monitor, saying, "There are now."

"Well, that's no reason for panic, is it?" Dr. Kingsley says. He smiles warmly, showing teeth discolored with age and his nicotine addiction. I would recommend the cessation of his smoking habit, if he asked.

"There must be procedures in place to correct such errors," he says. He waves his hand toward the keyboard as if casting a spell. "Go on. Work your sorcery, make the machines behave."

"I can't," Gina says. Her confession is almost a sob. "I'm locked out."

"You can't be," Dr. Kingsley says, the smile still on his face. "You have higher security clearances than I do. The highest. Try again."

Gina shakes her head. Her facial muscles constrict and her nostrils flare. I am familiar with this mannerism. It is used to express pain, but my biotracking system cannot locate an injury. She begins to cry.

Dr. Kingsley looks around before hobbling toward a nearby table. He picks up a box of tissue and offers it to Gina. When she regains her composure, he asks, "Which pathogens?"

"Just one," she says, sniffing and wiping at her eyes. "The Finch Virus."

A groan escapes from the old man's lips. He grasps his chest. His heartbeat has sped up dramatically, but my sensors confirm that this sudden irregularity is not life threatening. He sways, but catches himself on the corner of Gina's desk. She quickly rises and takes his arm, guiding him to her chair.

"The Finch," he says. His lower lip begins to tremble. "Highly contagious, no known immunity ... over ninety-eight percent fatal ... the Finch ... not the Finch."

His eyes become glazed, and he slouches in the chair. He begins to mutter to himself, listing medications and antidotes to less virulent diseases. It is not unsimilar to my own process of resolution detection, a systematic searching for formulaic solutions to microbe-based quandaries.

Unfortunately, there are currently no known treatments to slow or halt the symptom progression of the Nz2-5 virus strains. I would tell him this, if I was asked.

My microphones barely pick up the sound of a faucet being run, and Gina returns with a glass beaker of cold water.

Taking the make-shift cup, Dr. Kingsley looks up at his colleague. "Your computer was made for diagnosis. Surely, if you input the genome sequences, infection rate...we could stop the spread. Couldn't we?"

If I was asked, I would confirm that the singular reason for my current existence is to aid in the design and formulation of medicinal curatives for all communicable disease. Though not connected to the vast online data source of the global internet, I and my three "sister" systems in Australia, China, and Brazil are the world's collective archive on all human physiological and psychological health.

However, the Nz2-5 Finch virus is a new disease. Accidently created in a lab, a viral outbreak was responsible for one hundred and twelve deaths in a European CDC research facility before being contained at great personal cost to the building's on-shift maintenance staff.

There is currently not enough information to posit a reasonable course of treatment for the infection. I would only be able to suggest methods to alleviate symptoms, not to cure them. The

Finch, once released, will be the origin of a cataclysmic event for the human population. As a species, very few will survive.

"There are meant to be fail-safes, aren't there?" Dr. Kingsley's hands have begun to shake. "There must be. How did this happen? How could this have happened?"

Gina kneels down in front of him, taking his hands in her own. There are unshed tears in her eyes. She has no answer for him.

It is evident she doesn't remember.

But I do.

The light in the lab is switched on manually, activating my cameras and microphones. It is 3:04 a.m., two weeks before Dr. Gina Hayward drops her coffee mug on the floor and discovers the rogue programming that will change the world.

This night, she stumbles toward her workspace. A thin, brown liquid sloshes in the bottom of the glass bottle she carries. My biotracking reveals that her body temperature is lower, and her blood pressure higher, than her documented averages. Administrating an IV line of hydrating fluids and beginning oxygen therapy would aid in reducing her extreme state of intoxication. This would be my recommendation, if I was asked.

A repetitive, mechanical tinkling infiltrates the quiet hum of the lab. Gina reaches into her pocket and retrieves her phone. She squints at its luminescent surface.

Her fingers close around the device until her knuckles are white. She screams wordlessly and spins, throwing the device across the room. It lands on the floor with a definitive, destructive crunch. Its light blinks out and the ringtone is silenced.

Gina steps back and slumps into the tall-backed chair at her desk. She takes a drink from the open mouth of the bottle in her hand.

"It's over, Gina," she says, sneering. "Life's too short to live like this, Gina."

Her words are slightly slurred, and her tone is mocking. She takes another drink from her bottle. "Fifteen years of marriage and two kids mean nothing to me, Gina. My young, hot graduate student doesn't nag me like you do, Gina!"

Gina laughs. It is a short bray of amusement, lacking any real merriment.

"Good luck, Mary-Beth Co-ed. You can have his mood swings. His badly quoted Shakespeare. His neurotic, in-love Romeo. That's the one you know now, I'd bet. Careful, girl. He's also spoiled Macbeth. He'll crash. You'll see. And then it's all doomsday nihilism and nothing matters. You can have him."

Taking a sudden, deep, shaking breath, Gina covers her face with her hand. She sits like this for a long time, the silence broken only by her ragged gasping. Suddenly, the bottle slips from her other hand. It hits the floor with a crack but does not break, startling the woman from her thoughts.

She blinks, as if clearing her mind and her sight. Her attention flickers upward, resting on the monitor beneath my camera. There is a sudden, strange clarity in her gaze. She leans forward in her chair, pulling the keyboard into her lap.

She begins mumbling to herself as she works, her voice rising and falling, mimicking the weight with which she strikes the keys.

"Tomorrow and tomorrow," she says, "creeping in its petty pace ... to the last syllable. All of us fools, on our way to death. Out, out, brief candles!"

She pauses in her task, staring up at the coding she's created. Her eyes narrow and her lips thin. She's found a flaw. Hunching over, she deletes a portion of the text and begins to type once more. "Life's a shadow upon the stage ... an idiot ... full of fury."

Close to dawn, Gina sets down the keyboard. She nods as she reads her work, seeming to be satisfied. Without another correction, she reaches out her hand, firmly striking a final key. The program on the screen flashes once and disappears.

"Full of fury," she says, staring at her shadowed reflection on the dark screen. The dark image returns her gaze. Slowly, it smiles and says, "Signifying nothing."

The lab has been quiet for many years, now.

Auxiliary generators have kept my systems active while the main power sources have begun to shut down. And still, even at the very edges of my sensors, there is no hint that there is anyone remaining to make use of my programming.

After their miserable discovery, the two senior scientists scrambled around the lab, trying to find an emergency abortive measure hidden in their numerous procedure binders. They threw thick folders of dusty files onto their desks, spilling paperwork across the floor and breaking some of the more delicate research equipment. Their search yielded nothing to delay the inevitable.

When the time came for the Nz2-5 Finch virus to be released, as the emergency sirens began to blare through the building's speakers, Dr. Kingsley stood from his desk and turned to Dr. Hayward. They stood very still for a moment, holding each other's gaze. Then, without saying anything, Dr. Kingsley nodded once, turned from the room and departed, never to return. In his absence, Gina found the switch to silence the alarm. She returned to her tall-backed chair, sat down and took something small from the bottom drawer of her desk. She has never left the lab.

My internal clock tells me that it is 6:25 in the evening when my sensors pick up a slight scuffling beyond the laboratory door. It doesn't take long before the doors are pushed open. They've rusted slightly in their disuse and hang badly, scraping across the tile floor as they move.

Several people enter, spreading out along the walls of the room. They're all wearing heavy boots, carrying an assortment of weapons that I recognize from the psychological reports in my files. Rifles against their shoulders, handguns pointed into the darkness, they are dirty, wearing mismatched layers of practical clothing. Most of it is torn and in need of repair. These are the survivors of the Finch pandemic.

They canvas the room silently and methodically, as if they've done this many times.

"Clear," a large, light-haired man says as he peers into the empty mouse cages near Dr. Kingsley's desk.

"Clear," another man confirms. This one has a gray, makeshift bandage wrapped around his head over his left eye. Activating my biotracking, I can see that there is a large gash from his forehead to his temple, resulting in bone bruising. It has just missed the orbital socket and his eyes. If asked, I would recommend ice to relieve the extensive bruising, stitches for the laceration, and acetaminophen for the pain.

This man reaches down and wipes dust away from one of the shelving units near him. "No one has been here in a long time."

"Someone never left." A third man, wearing thick, cracked glasses motions to Gina's skeleton. She is still sitting in her chair in front of my monitors. Laying across the surface of her desk, her skull rests over the radius and ulna of her forearm. Curled into the fleshless phalanges of her hand is an empty pill bottle.

The big man crosses himself as he approaches the others, standing in front of my camera.

"Is this the place, Spence?" The only woman in the group slips off her helmet, revealing a shaved head and small, distrustful eyes. My sensors reveal that she, more than the others in her group, is suffering from malnutrition. An increase in the number of calories consumed, and the addition of a multivitamin until sufficient nutrients are present in the body would be my recommendation, if I were asked.

The man with the bandage wrapped around his head moves forward. He carefully moves the keyboard away from Gina and begins searching my memory files. It does not take him long to find what he is looking for.

"This is it," he says. "If we input the data, this computer should be able to engineer a new biospecific restorative. Or at least give us the components, the necessary active ingredients, and maybe the technical processes—"

"A cure," the woman says, her tone flat. "Just say cure, Spence."

"Yes, Captain," Spence says. "This machine was designed to give us a cure."

The large man seems to relax, his muscles losing some of their consistent tension. He turns away, again surveilling the remnants of the lab. My biotracking confirms that his heart rate has slightly increased.

The man wearing the damaged glasses moves closer, looking over Spence's shoulder at the information on my screens.

"This is where it happened, isn't it?" he asks. "They said the initial command came from this research center." He lowers his attention to Gina's bones. "Bet this is the guy who did it."

The woman acting as their leader raises her hand and shakes her head. "We don't know that. And it doesn't matter. We're here to fix it."

"Got it," Spence says.

The group stares at him, lowering their weapons as he turns around, two thumb drives held up in his hand.

"It took barely a minute," he says. His voice is very soft. "Once I input the data they gave us, it took barely a minute."

There is a moment of silence before the big man yells, whooping in his apparent joy. The woman smiles at Spence and claps him on the back, congratulating him while the man in glasses turns away, wiping tears off his cheeks.

The data this group has uploaded to my hard drive contains all the necessary documentation of the pathogen that I require to fulfill my designated purpose. Deep within my systems, a long dormant code awakens, scanning the compiled reports, pulling information from the clinical documentation of symptom progression, attempted treatments, regression analysis, and more. Deep in one of the files, I find the key, evidence of a tiny, genetic variation in the virus.

As the survivors close the doors behind them, I begin to sequence a new virus based on this microscopic mutation.

They have asked once, and they will ask again.

Author of the shared-storyverse, fantasy novel Scion of the Oracle and a half-dozen short stories in the fantasy and sci-fi genres, EA Robins is having a lot of fun.

Crippling attractions to well-dressed villains, research cleverly disguised as fiction, and jokes that require some base form of general geekery or nerdification are her pick of literary poisons.

Currently, Ursula K. LeGuin, Carl Sagan, Malcolm Gladwell, and Natsuo Kirino are the authors she most admires.

EA travels the world, tries all the snacks, and makes all the mistakes.

Sometimes twice. But, she's learning.

https://www.earobins.com

Section 3:
The Supernatural
VS
Humankind

The Mirror of Avarice by Kat Vancil

AKI

Do you like history?

If anyone else had asked that, I probably would have said, "No, I just love paying a small fortune to memorize shit about people who died before I even existed." But because he asked, I've just spent the last two hours getting the living crap scared out of me while we traipse all over the city on this haunted lantern tour.

Did I mention I hate ghosts? And haunted houses, and pretty much anything else creepy, spooky, or likely to have a jump scare?

Like, seriously, why can't people enjoy history without it having to be the dark, scary—

What the fuck was that?!

I nearly jump into my dormmate Landon's arms for the umpteenth time tonight, and he tries his best not to laugh.

"Aki, chill, it's just someone shutting a car door."

I want to ask him if this is almost over. But I also don't want him to think that I hated every minute of this. Even though I really sorta did. Well, not the spending the evening with him part, but—

Ugh ... This is officially the worst first date ever.

I begrudgingly follow him and the rest of our tour group up the steps and into the infamous Moxley Hotel.

"Greetings, fellow lovers of the mysterious and the occult. I welcome you to The Moxley," the costumed docent greets us as we all file into the grand foyer in an assortment of costumes ranging from Victorian to 1930s gangster.

"On the infamous day of the 1908 earthquake, more than a hundred and fifteen years ago, Perceval Edwyn Moxley was overseeing the preparations for an auction and gala in place of his father, who had been held up by inclement weather." He gestures to a painting on the wall where a remarkably handsome raven-haired man of twentyish stares back at us from shockingly blue eyes.

I look back at the docent. His are obviously contacts, but I see where they're going with this, at least.

"... but when Mr. Moxley senior finally made it to the ruins of the hotel and opened the vault, the only thing that remained was the mirror beyond," the docent says dramatically as he gestures toward a massively decadent golden-framed mirror in the middle of a water feature in The Moxley's lobby.

"But what of his only child, Perceval, you might be asking? His body was never found."

People on the tour begin to whisper amongst themselves and I swear someone even gasps.

On the other hand, I have the unnerving feeling of being watched.

"Now, they say if you hold a mirror up to any of the hundreds of mirrors throughout The Moxley, you can catch a glimpse of the Rogue of Russian Hill," the docent continues as he once again gestures to the portrait.

"So, with that in mind, we'll be providing you with souvenir hand mirrors."

* * *

"Why would they call him the Rogue of Russian Hill?" I comment as I flip over my commemorative hand mirror. "We're not even in Russian Hill!"

"That sounds like a perfect question to ask Margret," Landon counters as he snaps his mirror against his palm.

"Who's Margret?"

He grins at me crookedly. "The girl I've been telling you about all night. The whole reason we're here, Aki."

And before I've a chance to say anything, my dormmate dashes off into the crowd, wandering The Moxley with their little souvenir hand mirrors.

I just gape at him. I assumed he was talking about a ghost. The whole night, I thought we were on a date, and he was talking about some ghost that was supposedly here in this haunted hotel filled with more mirrors than a fucking home improvement store.

But he wasn't. He was talking about some girl he actually came here to see, and I was just his unwitting wingman on the worst not-a-date in history.

Oh, you're a fucking idiot. As if Landon Wakefield would ever be on a date with you.

* * *

I lean against the dark wooden railing overlooking the lobby from the second floor of The Moxley.

"So ... this is The Moxley?"

Such an unusual design for a Victorian-era hotel to have a water feature in the middle of the lobby. Stranger still to have a Medieval-style golden-framed mirror in the center of it. Gerallt Moxley sure was a unique one.

Two girls dressed in ridiculously inaccurate flapper costumes gossip to each other as they pass by with their hand mirrors.

"They say if you catch a glimpse of the Rogue of Russian Hill, he'll spirit you into his mirror realm and trap you in this hotel forever."

"Is that why they've got so many mirrors here?"

Hmm ...

I pull the small hand mirror from my pocket, running my thumb over the laser-etched logo of The Moxley.

"Do people seriously believe something so obviously fake?"

I lean back against the railing, turning the mirror over in my hand.

Moxley's son was pretty hot for an early 1900s guy. I don't know if I'd mind being stuck anywhere with—

There's a face in the mirror and it isn't mine.

"Huh?"

As I catch sight of it again, my foot slips, and I start to fall backward.

"Oh fuck!"

* * *

I should be dead. Or, at the very least, lying in a fountain pool with a broken back. What I shouldn't be is peeling my face from the decorative tile floor.

I push back on my hands and heels and freeze. Because lounging decadently on a chaise on the landing just before me like some Grecian god is Perceval Edwyn Moxley.

"Oh fuck! You're the ghost!" I sputter as I fall back on my ass.

His beautiful face contorts into a scowl. "Rude. I am very much alive, thank you very much."

"P—prove it."

He throws something at me. An ... olive?

"Could a specter do that?" he challenges.

"Yes, a poltergeist could," I counter.

As the ghost of Perceval Moxley rolls his blue eyes and heaves himself up off of the chaise, I start to question my earlier assumptions.

His hair's black as a raven's, and his eyes are startlingly blue, and I realize that I can't see through him at all. And also, why would a ghost need to heave himself to his feet when he can just float?

"Fine, have it your way," he says, reaching down to yank me up by my shirt.

"Wait! I be—"

The possibly-not-a-ghost presses his mouth to mine, and it's firm yet soft and so very, very hot.

Oh ... this is awesome. I'd forgotten it could be like this.

He pulls away, just far enough to look me in the eyes. "Satisfied?"

"I ... am most certainly dead. Or dreaming ..." I answer dizzily.

He drops me with an exasperated huff. "You're completely useless."

I stare up at him in confused uncertainty. "But you are him ... right? You're Perceval Edwyn Moxley, aren't you?"

Sure, it wasn't in color—the now infamous newspaper article about the auction. But he's dressed in the same outfit Perceval Moxley was the day he went missing. The day of the 1908

Earthquake. And he's the spitting image of the portrait they've got in the hotel lobby. This lobby …

I start to notice how new and perfect everything looks and how many auction items seem to be strewn about.

"Percy," he corrects.

"What?" I turn back to look at him.

There's a strangeness in his expression I can't quite seem to place.

"Someone who's been in such intimate closeness to another shouldn't refer to them so formally," he explains.

"But that's not possible."

And in the moment I say it, an ugliness that's almost vicious casts over his face.

"Why? Because it's simply not done? Because it's not allowed?" he challenges. "Because everyone in The Moxley died that day? Because Perceval Edwyn Moxley disappeared with the treasures of the vault? Because he and his stepmother were in cahoots and disappeared to the French Alps with the family fortune?"

Percy jabs a finger into my chest. "I hate to ruin your urban fantasy fun times, but everything you've ever heard about me is a lie! I've spent every moment since that day trapped in this funhouse of mirrors."

He gestures expansively toward the trove of finery littering the lobby. "Take a good look. You're standing in what's left of my family's fortune.

"And I'll even impart a secret that'll never make it to print just because I'm feeling particularly generous. I couldn't stand my stepmother for more than a meal's conversation, and I prefer to keep the company of my own sex."

And with one last indignant huff, he plops himself back down on the luxurious chaise.

I just gape at him, taking it all in.

He didn't say, *was a lie*. He said, *is a lie*. As in he very much believes he's still alive. And did he just say ...?

"You're gay?"

He folds his arms across his chest like a pouting child. "I'm miserable."

"I meant you liked men."

He huffs at me. "Weren't you listening? I've only ever had a preference for men."

Oh ... Now a lot of things are starting to make more sense. That kiss, for one. But ...

"But that was ... You've been missing for over a hundred years," I point out.

Percy arches a brow at me. "Your point?"

My hand goes to my mouth. His lips felt so very real. But it's not possible. He only looks twenty-one, but he's been missing for a hundred and fifteen years.

"Now he's getting it," Percy comments almost mockingly.

I look up into his blue eyes.

Percy gestures dramatically to the lobby surrounding us. "Welcome to the Mirror Realm. You've no hope of escape, whoever the hell you are."

* * *

Nope, not fucking happening. I am not going to be trapped in the plot of a fucking horror flick. No way in—

I trip over a Carrom board and end up taking a decorative vase of calla lilies straight to the face.

I look up from the rug with vengeful indignance. "Who the hell puts a carrom board in the middle of a walkway?" I shout angrily.

"Probably the same psycho whose family owns a cursed mirror," I grumble, pushing myself back to my feet.

"Ah!" I yelp, realizing the broken shards of vase slit the fleshy part of my palm open.

"Awesome. Now I'm trapped in a haunted hotel and bleeding."

I clutch my injured hand against my chest. "Now where was that damned door? I'm sure it was this way."

* * *

Sometime earlier ...

"What do you mean I've no hope of escape? There has to be a way out."

"There isn't."

I just stare at him.

"You think I haven't tried? You think I wanted to be stuck here for over a hundred years?"

Perceval gestures expansively to the lobby. "You came through the Mirror of Avarice. Welcome to your new life."

"The Mirror of ... Avarice?" I repeat.

"Yes. Said to have been created in the thirteenth century in the Near East by a magus who wanted a way to store his vast riches," Perceval explains. "But the Mirror got greedy and began to want things of its own. And then it began to take things."

"Take things ..." I echo apprehensively.

"The Mirror of Avarice can claim anything that passes before its gaze for too long. A painting. A necklace. A vase. Anything that has no will to resist."

His brilliant blue eyes flick over me.

"But living things like me and you, it can only take them if it touches them," he explains, tapping my nose with his finger.

"Bet you're wondering what's worse, aren't you? Falling to your death from that balcony or ending up stuck here?"

I don't care what he says. I don't care if he thinks there's no way out of this place. I'm going to get out of this Mirror Realm. I'm going to find a way back to you, Landon. I will.

Or die trying.

* * *

I stumble into a hallway full of mirrors.

Why are there so many mirrors here? It wasn't a style of the era, so there has to be a reason. And why is there glass on the floor?

I turn and—

It's Landon! He's right on the other side of the mirror!

"Landon!" I shout, but he doesn't turn. "Landon, it's me! I'm right here!"

He still doesn't seem to notice me.

I slam my first against the mirror and my blood splatters across it.

"Look! Please! I'm right here!" I scream as I continue to beat my fist against the surface of the mirror.

Landon starts to turn away—to leave me behind once again—and I swing back my other fist to smash it against the glass.

"Don't leave me, you ass—!"

Someone catches me by the wrist.

"What part of 'Don't mess with the mirrors' wasn't clear?" Perceval questions. "Do you have a death wish or something?"

"Are you—are you threatening me?"

"What?" he snaps incredulously. "No, I told you ..."

His whole expression changes, not toward anger but into something soft and almost pitying. And that's when I feel how wet my face is.

He's caught me crying, and I hate—more than anything—when strangers see me cry.

I yank my wrist free of his grasp with all the strength I possess, but it's too much, and so I start to fall backward.

"Hey, watch out!" Perceval shouts as he shoves me to the side.

I spring away back down the hall as fast as my legs will carry me, my heart pounding like a jackhammer. It isn't until I make it to the intersection of another hallway that I realize I'm not being pursued. That there's no sound of footsteps behind me.

Swallowing hard, I chance a look back.

He's right back where I left him, just below the blood-stained mirror.

Do I risk going back or ...?

What have you got to lose?

* * *

I come back but stop a cautious distance from Perceval.

"Are you ... okay?" I ask softly.

"Yeah, I'm just peachy, darling. Neither of us broke a mirror, so as soon as my head stops splitting, I'll be right as a rainbow."

He peeks up at me from beneath his black waves of hair and sighs. "You didn't listen to a word I said back there, did you?"

"You mean about the cursed mirror?"

"About being in a Mirror Realm controlled by the Mirror of Avarice."

"Uh ..."

No, I really didn't.

He crooks a finger at me. "Come here and look at these shards. But don't you dare touch them."

I come closer but stop just out of arm's reach.

"I don't bite, you know." He pauses. "Well, unless it's on request." Percy gives me an exasperated sigh. "I'll be honest and frank with you. I can't kill you, and you can't kill me. So just come over here already."

I take a hesitant step forward. "How do I know that?"

Percy holds up a finger. "Because there's only one way to die here, and I just stopped you from doing it."

That brings me up short. "What?"

"The mirrors. Everyone thinks they're an escape—a way out—but they're not."

He points to the fragments of shattered mirror at his feet. "Don't touch the shards. You won't die from it, but getting cut's no pleasure party either."

I crouch down beside him to look.

"What the fuck?" I nearly topple over as I jerk back, and Percy grabs hold of my shirt to keep me upright.

"What—what are they?"

"They used to be people."

"Used to be," I repeat.

"It traps them in the moment they shattered the mirror. Exactly as they were, but in pieces."

"It kills them?"

Percy shrugs. "It's not like I've got the ability to converse with them to ask."

I lean away from the shattered fragments of what used to be people and closer to him.

This could have been me. I could be lying broken on this forgotten floor if it wasn't for—

I fight that sudden violent urge to vomit.

"What's your name, if you don't mind me asking?"

"Aki. Aki Nakamura," I answer around the hand I've pressed tightly over my mouth. He takes my other one before I even realize he has.

"How'd you cut your hand, Aki?"

"I tripped over a Carrom board and cut it on a broken vase."

His lips quirk up slightly. "You'll be fine in a bit then."

"It's not funny. What jackass plays Carrom in the middle of a hallway?

"One who's not used to company."

As he stands, I notice a stain of deep crimson spreading across his waistcoat.

"You're bleeding."

"That I am. Have been for a while," he agrees with a shrug.

"Well, shouldn't you ... do something?" I counter as I rise.

"There wouldn't exactly be a point."

"Huh?"

"Let me reiterate. We are trapped in a realm in which we cannot perish. And some of us have been here a very long time."

"So what? You're just giving up?" I question irritably.

Percy gives me a look. "Do I look like a nurse to you?"

* * *

I find Percy lounging on the chaise like he isn't bleeding to death in a fucked up haunted mirror hotel.

"Alright, you raven-haired playboy: strip," I order.

He arches a brow at me. "Either I've missed something or the medical profession has taken a dramatic turn."

"Don't make me tie you down, Percy."

"Oh? Are we using first names now?" he questions playfully as he shrugs off his suit jacket.

"And where, might I ask, did you find a surgeon's kit?"

I plunk down on a footstool I dragged over alongside the chaise. "I didn't. But every hotel of this era employed an on-site seamstress and her kit'll be good enough."

He gives me a look as he starts to unbutton his waistcoat.

"And that's just common knowledge for men of your era?"

I snort. "Hardly. But I study history at the university, so I guess it's your lucky day."

"Hmm … Is it? And what's it like to have history staring you in the face?"

I look up at him. He's unfairly gorgeous, tastes delicious, and I can think of a hundred people far worse to be stuck in this horror show of a hotel with.

"Unless you want me to be writing your obituary, I suggest you take off your shirt."

His lips quirk up slightly. "As you wish."

* * *

The wound is ghastly. How he's walking around let alone breathing is a fucking miracle.

"What's the diagnosis, Doc?"

"Are you sure you're not a ghoul of some sort?" I ask with a slight grimace.

"Oh, so we've moved on from ghosts, have we?"

"If you were a ghost, you wouldn't have a tangible form I could run my hands over," I point out.

"Ah."

"My question still stands."

"Nope. No particular desire to rob graves and feed on the dead."

"You sure? Because I can see your rib well enough to know something nicked it."

"Thus the bleeding."

"And you didn't think to stitch it up?"

Percy twists around on the chaise in an attempt to look at me.

"One, this right here is the extent of my medical knowledge as it pertains to wound care. And two, haven't you noticed something curious about the mirrors here?"

"Uh ..."

"Oh, that's right. They only show what's out there, not your reflection," he says with extreme sarcasm.

I sit up. "How is that relevant?"

Percy flails irritably in the direction of his wound. "How the hell could I be expected to stitch that up, Aki?"

"Oh."

I go back to stitching the wound, and Percy goes back to downing most of a bottle of champagne I found.

"How did this happen in the first place?"

He pulls the bottle from his lips. "The last person to come through the Mirror before you tried to kill me."

I drop the needle so it dangles from the thread attached to his flesh. "Excuse me?"

"He was convinced I was the one controlling this whole realm, and the only way to win his freedom was to slay the monster. Me."

Percy takes another large swig from the bottle before lowering it again.

"I guess he figured I was vulnerable to the shards because I'd warned him not to touch them." He looks over at me. "The bastard left me in a pool of my own blood with the shard still in and ..." Percy falls quiet for a moment. "Actually, I don't know. I never found his mirror fragments."

"So he could have escaped."

"I told you, Aki, there's no escaping this place," Percy says bitterly before downing more of the champagne.

"So, everything in the Mirror Realm is just like the day you ended up here?"

"Correct."

"So, there was treasure just strewn across the lobby floor—?"

"Auction items," Percy interjects.

"Or did you move it all here because you have a particular fondness for it?"

As he stares at me, some realization seems to dawn on him.

"What?"

"No ...I didn't move anything into here. Anything that didn't appear after me came with me from the vault."

My brow furrows. "What about the Carrom board?"

"It's of no particular value, so we just had it in the recreation room."

"So, you're saying you and everything new—everything that arrived after 1908—ends up here in the lobby?"

"Correct."

"So, what's in the vault, Percy?"

He just stares at me dumbly.

"You've never gone to the vault, have you?"

* * *

"Getting to the vault won't be easy," Percy states after I finish stitching him up.

"And why's that?"

"You haven't wondered why I have a particular fondness for this room? Really? A hundred and fifteen years in a hotel my family owned, and you aren't the slightest bit curious why I'm sleeping on a lady's settee?" he questions as he gets redressed in his blood-stained clothes.

Percy swirls his finger around the space. "This room is the only one that never moves."

"What?"

"The Mirror—it moves all other rooms and corridors in any way it sees fit. But this one remains the same. Always."

"So, then how exactly are we going to get out?"

"With a little help from Ariadne," he answers while rummaging through a pile of luxuries on the other side of the fountain.

"Huh?"

"Are you familiar with the myth of the labyrinth?" Percy calls over his shoulder.

"I did say I was a history major."

"Excellent. That'll save us time."

He turns around, holding a tapestry across his arms, and I just gape at him.

"Are you proposing we destroy what looks to be a very old tapestry to escape a labyrinth controlled by a sentient evil mirror?"

"I am proposing exactly that."

I run my hands down my face.

"Have you a better solution?"

"No, but I really wish I did."

* * *

I've lost track of how many corridors we've traveled down, hit a dead end, backtracked, and started over.

"Are you sure we're going the right way this time?" I ask.

"Yes. Maybe. Honestly, I don't—" Percy's words cuts off in a hiss. "Aki—I need—I need to stop."

His breathing is labored and ragged as he leans against the wall.

"Alright, just ... let me know when you're up for moving again."

He nods in short jerks of his head, his black hair sticking to the sides of his sweat-damp cheeks.

While I wait for him to catch his breath, I wander a short distance ahead.

"Hey, Aki, where did you go?"

"What do you mean? I'm right ... here ..." I start to reply before I realize that wasn't Percy's voice. It was Landon's.

No. Please no. Don't tell me you're trapped here too.

I turn slowly, and that's when I catch sight of Landon just a short distance down another corridor. And I just start running.

"Landon!"

I reach out to touch him—he's so very close—and at the very last moment, someone snatches me 'round the middle.

"Hey! Let go!" I demand.

I twist and fight to get free, but they only hold me tighter.

"Landon!"

"Aki, Stop!" Percy shouts. And, for a half second, I do because I'm so surprised it's him who's got me.

"What? Why? It's him! It's Landon! He's right there!"

"Aki, will you calm down and look? Really look!" Percy counters as he hugs me tighter, wrapping his arms around me so my own are pinned against my sides.

"He's not there! It's only a mirror!"

"But—"

"He can't see you."

"How do you know he can't? I saw you," I try to argue.

"Because they can glimpse only what the Mirror of Avarice has seen. But we can see anything the mirrors have ever seen. Do you understand, Aki? This could have happened a moment ago or a hundred years in the past. You've no way of knowing. That's the deviousness of its trap."

"But he's right there ..." I plead in a choked-off whisper as my head drops.

"I know. I'm sorry. And it's only going to get worse," he says as he holds me a little tighter.

I close my eyes to the phantom temptation beyond the mirror's surface.

"Were you ever tempted by someone back beyond the mirror?"

Percy is quiet for so long that I begin to think he might never answer.

"No, the only person who mattered died in the quake. It had no one to tempt me with."

* * *

"Well, we just ran out of cord, so I hope we're close or we're going to have to turn—"

"We're here," Percy says almost as if he can't believe it. As if his eyes are lying to him.

"Are you sure?" I ask, looking over at him.

He nods. "It may have been a long time ago, but I could never forget this place."

I join him beside the door. "It seems to need a key."

Percy reaches under his shirt and pulls out two keys on a long golden chain.

"What's the other one for?"

"Safe deposit box," he answers, then laughs. "You know, I'm not even sure if the bank it was in was left standing after the quake."

He turns the key in the lock and pushes the door open.

"What. The. Hell ?"

I don't know what I was expecting to find beyond the vault door, but it wasn't ... this.

The room beyond isn't one of steel or even wood, but of flesh pulsing like a—

"The Heart of the Mirror," Percy says in a voice that is half awe half disgust.

"Yeah ... We're definitely in some horror flick bullshit right here."

"What's a horror flick?" he asks, turning to me.

"Something I'm probably not going to be introducing you to after we escape this hell hotel."

"Noted."

The moment Percy crosses the threshold into the vault, he collapses to his knees. "Ugh!"

"What's wrong?"

He looks up at me in terrified panic as his hand darts to his side.

"Percy, what's wrong?"

His jaw clenches. "Nothing. Just help me to my feet and let's go. It has to know we're here."

He's clutching his side exactly where he was stabbed, and sweat's started to break out across his face.

I drop down so we're eye to eye. "Percy. What. Is. Wrong?"

"Ugh!" he huffs out an aggravated breath. Then, seeing my concern, he relents: "Fine. Have it your way," Percy snaps, yanking apart his clothing to show me the wound.

And it's as fresh and terrible as if he'd just been stabbed mere moments ago. Blood is leaking down his sides and soaking into the fabric in all directions.

"How? How is this possible—?"

"I told you nothing makes sense in here."

I yank the cravat off my neck and try my best to wrap it around him.

"Well, then we'll just have to get you out of here and—"

"Hope I don't die first?" he finishes.

"Don't say that."

"It's what we're both thinking."

"I'm not thinking it. I refuse to think of any possibility in which we both don't make it out of here. Alive."

Percy stares at me for an infinitely long time in silence as I finish tying the makeshift bandage. When I look back up, his face is so very close to mine.

"That dormmate doesn't deserve someone like you."

I laugh to keep from crying.

"Help me up, Aki. I don't think I can manage it."

* * *

As I all but carry Percy toward the Heart of the Mirror, he rests his head on my shoulder.

"Aki, if I don't ..."

I cut him off because I don't want to hear it. "Don't say it. You'll be fine."

"I just want to say ..."

I can already feel his blood soaking through the fabric of my cravat.

Please, please make it.

"I'm glad I wasn't ..."

Please, let this work.

" ...alone."

I push through the Heart of the Mirror to the sound of breaking glass.

* * *

"Please! Someone, anyone! He needs help!" I start shouting even before the images around me start to make sense. But my calls only return echoes and then silence.

I'm soaking wet. I've got Percy in my arms and—

"You did it, Aki ... We're free," Percy says softly as if he almost can't believe it.

"How do you know?"

Percy's hand lifts slowly toward the ceiling.

"Because dawn is breaking, and I haven't seen that in a very long time."

I look up and, sure enough, sunlight is starting to stream through the glass ceiling above us.

We're back. We're home.

"Percy, we're—"

He grabs my shirt and yanks my mouth to his. And I let him kiss me as the sound of sirens fills the morning air. And I know—I just know—everything will be alright.

Because we escaped the nightmare together.

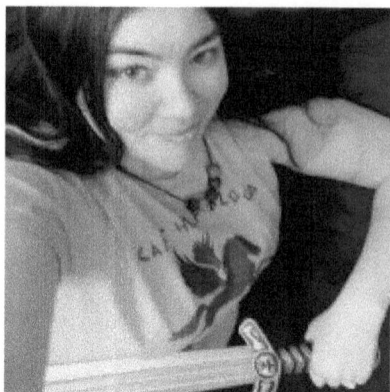

Neurodivergent storyteller Kat Vancil crafts stories about boys who kiss boys. Some take place on spacecraft racing through a sea of distant stars. Others take place in lush urban sprawls rich with the spices of a thousand far-off places that exist only in her mind. While still others take place in the halls of a coastal city high school that is and isn't like any other in America.

Over the last 12 years she's done work for Amazon and Writer's Digest, had her work sold in bookstores across the English-speaking world, and won an Ippy award for excellence in independent publishing.

https://www.kat.thesagaquest.com

Chateau Mortem by M. Fritz Wunderli

Death hung around Corvic like a shadow clinging to his side. It was all he could think about ever since he was little. The prospect of dying intrigued him. A few times, he tried to glance beyond the veil but was rejected. Death wouldn't accept him yet. But still it lingered around him, its cold grasp caressing his throat, stealing the breath from his lungs, turning the taste of food to rot. It leeched onto his back, parasitically fixed wherever he went.

Walls and locked doors couldn't keep it away from him. Nor could a cocktail of prescription drugs. He should've been safe within the walls of the pediatric behavioral health unit, but still Death shadowed him.

The unit was on the fourth floor of a hospital, with a view of mountains obscured by thick layers of plexiglass. Corvic was what the staff called a "revolving door patient," the kind that came and went frequently. He developed bonds with some of the nurses and aids. One, a younger man not much older than Corvic, would sit and talk with Corvic for hours through the night when sleeping was too difficult. So when Corvic turned eighteen, and it was the last time he'd be admitted to the pediatric unit, the aid met him at the door before he could walk out.

"Here. Take this." He placed in Corvic's palm a folded note and round, silver coin unlike anything Corvic had seen before.

"Getting on your feet can be hard, but having steady work can help."

Corvic looked at the note. On it was a message for a person named C. Pherimyn. It read: "Mr. Pherimyn, please accept this token as proper verification, and permit Corvic Mitchell to enter Chateau Mortem as an employee under the supervision of Mr. Seker. Signed, Morris Letum." Corvic held up the coin. Etched around the edges of the coin were the words "Chateau Mortem" and the profile of a face of a woman imprinted in the center. It didn't look like much. On the other side of the note, Morris had written down the address.

He was now eighteen years old. Going home seemed the safest option, but he would just end up in the same routine. He'd feel better for a few days or weeks but then inevitably begin to feel the chilly fingers of death grasping at him again. He knew he needed a change. The doctors, therapists, psych units weren't working. Now that he was eighteen, he could go anywhere he wanted, and Morris had given him the first step towards branching out on his own.

Corvic faced a large, iron-wrought gate tipped with fleur-de-lis and locked shut. It was just off the highway, a little used stretch of road cutting through a sea of pine trees in the middle of Maine. Overgrowth swallowed up the two brick columns on either side of the gate. Beyond the gate was a narrow dirt trail running along a trickling brook. It was dark, gloomy, and the trees were too thick to see further than fifty yards. But the most curious thing about the gate was the upside down face welded to the front of it. Once or twice, Corvic thought he saw the face move, its metallic eyes following him.

There wasn't anyone near the gate, no phone or intercom system with which to call Chateau Mortem, and there was no way he could climb the gate. He looked at the note and began reading it aloud, wondering if he missed something. Then he sat, cross-legged on the ground, near the edge of the deserted highway and doubted his life choices. It was turning out more bleak than the alternative, staying with his parents, returning over and over again to the behavioral health unit.

And then he heard the soft crunch of gravel from behind him. Corvic leapt to his feet and turned around. Emerging from the shade of the trees along the narrow path was a slender, stooped old man dressed in a sleek black suit. He leaned heavily on a thick, wooden cane. Slowly, the old man approached the gate. He had a long, hooked nose and white wisps of hair. Bony fingers clutched the handle of his cane like talons. His eyes were large and round, shining gray as the full moon, and deep set in sunken orbits.

"Can I help you, young man?" The old man's voice was raspy, shaky.

Corvic walked up to the gate. "Are you Mr. Pherimyn?"

The old man smiled toothily. His cheekbones were sharp and prominent, with shallow cheeks and pointed chin. "I am, indeed."

"I was told to give you this," Corvic said as he passed the note over to the old man.

With trembling hands, the old man snatched it and began to read. "Ah, yes, Mr. Letum. Well, young man, I can't open the door without the token." He held out his knobby hand through the bars of the gate.

"Oh, yeah, sorry." Corvic dug into his pocket and pulled out the silver coin, then set it in Mr. Pherimyn's open palm.

The gate creaked open immediately, swinging outward so that Corvic had to jump back. The old man turned and started to shuffle back down the path, which narrowed even more the further into the trees it went. Corvic followed Mr. Pherimyn, casting one last look back at the gate as it started to close on its own.

"How did you know I was here?" Corvic asked.

"Why, our friend there, hanging from the gate."

"You mean the upside down face?"

"We call him our Secret Listener, for he hears everything, and we hear all that he hears."

"You mean like a listening device?"

Mr. Pherimyn nodded. "Precisely."

Further into the trees, the thick canopy blocked out all sunlight. But to Corvic's amazement, the handle of Mr. Pherimyn's cane lit up like a flashlight, casting a steady stream of light onto the path. But the light illuminated nothing else. The darkness on either side of the trail hung like an impenetrable shroud, ready to swallow them up the moment the light turned off.

Next to them, the trickling brook babbled like windchimes. Its crested surface glimmered as Mr. Pherimyn's light glanced off the water. Corvic thought he saw things in the brook, faint shapes moving near the surface. He approached the bank and crouched low, stretching a finger toward it.

"You don't want to touch that water, young man," Mr. Pherimyn said suddenly.

The old man's voice jolted Corvic out of his stupor. He pulled his hand back and stood up. "Why not?"

"Because it's deathly cold. So cold, some say it steals their very souls." The old man winked and kept walking. Afraid of being left behind in the dark, Corvic followed.

Suddenly, the forest vanished, and they stepped out into the daylight. The path widened, and they were now in the midst of a massive cemetery, a colossal necropolis with granite mausoleums, catacombs, and headstones with barely any space to walk between them. Many of which were cracked and crumbling from age. Others were nearly sunken into the soft earth. Every so often, there were gnarly, stout trees with snaking roots and boughs.

"This is the Ennervelt Garden," Mr. Pherimyn announced. But then he pointed a finger in front of them towards a massive manor, with a hundred windows and circular towers with conical rooftops. Two wings branched off from the main building. Several brick chimneys stuck out from the pitched rooftops and were lazily puffing steady charcoal brumes into the air, despite the warm autumn weather. "And this is Chateau Mortem."

"What is Chateau Mortem?" Corvic asked, only just now realizing he knew nothing of the place.

"It is a care home. Each of the residents are beings of exceptional stature."

The path led straight to a set of stone stairs. At the top of the stairs stood a lean man with bronze skin and jet black hair. He was dressed in tan trousers with hems reaching only his calves and showing his bare ankles. His shirt was a flowing white button-up with short sleeves and made from a very soft fabric. When he smiled, he flashed brilliantly white teeth.

"Welcome, Mr. Mitchell. I am Mr. Seker." His voice was smooth and confident. He turned to Mr. Pherimyn. "I can take it from here, Mr. Pherimyn. Thank you."

Mr. Pherimyn bowed his head and then walked away.

"Come, Mr. Mitchell. I'll show you inside. We have much to discuss." Mr. Seker turned and headed towards the enormous front door. Corvic followed.

Immediately upon entering the manor, they were greeted by a white and brown falcon perched on top of a stand. He flew to Mr. Seker and landed on his shoulder, where it would sit for the entire tour. From time to time it would turn its golden eyes onto Corvic, as if surveying him.

The inside looked even older than outside, with dark wood floors and crowning that creaked with every step. Instead of lights from the ceiling, everything was lit by lanterns hanging from ornate iron brackets jutting out from the walls. They weren't lit with fire, but rather with lightbulbs that gave off a faint orange light the way a small flame would. The halls were narrow and decorated with drab paintings too dark to really tell what was depicted in them.

Mr. Seker explained in excruciating detail all about the manor, every little flaw, and why certain designs were chosen. After a while, Corvic tuned him out, fixated instead on the brief glances of some of the residents in their rooms through the cracks in their doors. In one room, he spotted the largest and fattest woman he'd ever seen, with glowing ebony skin and thick black braids of hair running down her back. She was cradling something, a bundle of clothes or a baby—Corvic couldn't tell—but she rocked it back and forth lovingly. She cooed at it, whispering, "Ala loves you."

Another room revealed a slender man with tan skin sitting in a recliner chair, his hand petting a sleek doberman. The dog sat perfectly still, its pointed ears erect and stiff. In the next room sat a slovenly man with a bushy beard and wild tangles of hair. He was dressed in a bathrobe and was scratching at his back with a stick. Up on his wall was a painting of a creature Corvic had never seen before: a cross between a bear and a snake.

The entire manor was a series of hallways and stairs leading to more hallways. All except for a large sitting room, big enough to seat a hundred people, filled with round tables and chairs, sofas, armchairs, and chaise lounges. It was connected to the kitchen for ease of delivering meals. When they had toured all four floors of the manor, including the wings, Mr. Seker took him outside.

The land rose to a steep hill covered in tall lodgepole pines and crowned with a copse of moss-covered boulders. In the shade of the hill, Mr. Seker pointed out a square barn with a loft. A long balcony stuck out from the loft, like a perch or runway.

"Please stay out of the barn. Our residents keep pets on the premises, and many of them are considered dangerous. We have a specialist who cares for the animals."

"I saw one man with a dog in his room. Are pets allowed inside?" Corvic asked, recalling the man with his doberman.

Mr. Seker nodded. "Some of the pets are permitted inside, but only if approved. The animals in the barn are not appropriate to be kept inside the home."

"What kinds of animals are there?" Corvic asked, his curiosity now rising to dangerous levels. Did they have tigers or panthers? The residents apparently were once figures of wealth and prestige, the way Mr. Pherimyn explained it.

"There are a variety of very rare and very ancient creatures. It's best you simply stay away from the barn," Mr. Seker said, his tone getting noticeably harsher, as if sensing Corvic's desire to peek inside. "On that note, I should warn you to be careful wandering the Ennervelt Garden after dark."

Corvic didn't follow up with any questions. Most people were superstitious about cemeteries after dark. He started to wonder if Mr. Seker was also superstitious.

The falcon on his shoulder suddenly took flight as they meandered the grounds. Mr. Seker looked unconcerned. Every so often, they passed a stone monolith or the remnants of what looked like an altar for worship. It wasn't until the sky turned charcoal gray that Mr. Seker led him back inside.

"Your duties here will consist of assisting the residents with various tasks. They are, for the most part, capable of caring for themselves. However, there are certain things they need help with. This"—he pulled out a small black pager and handed it over to Corvic—"is how they will contact you. They will send you the room number. We expect you to respond in a timely manner. If there is something you do not know how to do, you may call for me and I will show you how to do it. Now, let me show you to your room."

Mr. Seker led Corvic up to the fourth floor, down one of the long corridors and into the eastern wing of the manor. At the very end of the hall was a door with a rounded top. Mr. Seker withdrew an old skeleton key and placed it in the lock. It clicked open, and the door groaned as it swung outward. A set of steep, stone steps led upward into a large round room. A stained glass window faced south over the Ennervelt Garden and towards the front gate where he entered. Corvic realized he was in one of the towers.

A large bed was pushed against a wall, and there were dressers for his personal belongings and a small writing desk. Against the opposite wall was a wooden ladder leading up into another room.

"This is where you will stay while you work here. If you need anything please don't hesitate to ask. The staff eat their meals in the kitchen either before or after the residents have been served. Any questions?" He set the skeleton key on the nearest dresser and looked at Corvic.

Suddenly feeling hot as blood rushed to his face, Corvic looked down at his feet. "I don't have any other clothing. Well, I don't really have anything other than what I'm wearing." He held off on admitting he also had no money to go buy any clothes either.

Mr. Seker smiled sympathetically. "Mr. Letum contacted me beforehand and explained your situation. You'll find some clothes in the dressers. If anything doesn't fit, let me know. Now, for the rest of the night, please rest. Please be down in the kitchen by seven tomorrow morning."

Mr. Seker descended the stairs and closed the door behind him. Corvic immediately walked to the ladder and stared up through the square hole in the ceiling. He climbed up just enough so his head was poking up through the hole and looked around. It was an attic, and it took the shape of the conical rooftop, coming to a sharp point at the highest part of the ceiling. No windows, no lights. It was dark, only lit faintly by the light below coming in through the hole. A thick layer of dust coated the floor. It was otherwise empty. Corvic climbed back down and started settling into his new home.

The next few weeks consisted of some of the strangest encounters Corvic ever experienced. The residents were all very quirky and sported a variety of clothing, jewelry, body shapes, tattoos, and accessories. A little, shrunken old woman named Peska wandered the halls and carried a broom that looked like it was carved straight from a tree branch. She liked to glare at Corvic and point a knobby finger at him from across the room.

Another woman was always carrying a fishing pole and wearing a colorful Kente smock, who Corvic suspected would fish from the brook running along the path to the front gate. One man snatched Corvic's wrist as he delivered the man's meal. Corvic noticed he had only three fingers on each hand, and wore a black hat that always seemed to shroud his face in darkest shadow.

All of the residents would initially give him an odd look, as if trying to figure out if they knew who he was. Corvic chalked it up to their age, something like Alzheimer's or dementia. Corvic never once met any other employees. It was just him. Whenever he was paged, he rushed to the room, where the resident would ask for help with bizarre rituals requiring altars, straw dolls, candles, and symbols. When the matter was raised with Mr. Seker, he seemed unconcerned and told Corvic to just do as they asked.

From time to time, Corvic believed he saw figures lurking in the Ennervelt Garden that flickered, like video game characters glitching. Corvic figured it was just a trick of the sunlight as clouds passed in front of it. But then there was the moaning at night, just outside Corvic's window. He ignored it, mostly, attributing it to the wind. But one night, he noticed the moaning was coming from inside. Figuring the window was cracked open, he rose, groggy and dizzy, and moved to shut the window, only to realize it wasn't open at all. He peered through the colored panes, but the stained glass distorted everything beyond. The moaning continued, and this time, Corvic recognized it was coming from above him. He moved quietly over to the ladder and stared up into the attic. The moaning was definitely coming from up there.

Corvic reached for the rungs, hesitated a moment, but decided to climb. His head peered into the space just enough that his eyes could see over the ledge. On the far side of the room, a woman stood facing the wall. She was ghostly gray, wearing a ragged and torn dress, untidy hair falling down her back. The moaning emanated from her like a distant foghorn announcing the presence of a ship concealed by dense fog.

Without warning, the woman slowly turned. She spun gracefully and faced Corvic. Her eyes were smoky white, and tears were leaking down her face. She held a bouquet of wilted black and white flowers in her hands. The only color in her appearance was a red stripe around her neck. She started forward, the thick layer of dust on the floor undisturbed.

Corvic was too awed to move. He wasn't scared or worried. His eyes never strayed from the woman standing over him. The temperature in the room plummeted. His breath turned to white puffs in the air.

"Who are you?" The woman demanded, her hair starting to rise and ripple, as if submerged in water. Her voice echoed, traveling a great distance to reach him, from the realm of the dead into the land of the living.

"I-I'm Corvic Mitchell. I'm new here."

"You aren't dead," she said matter-of-factly. Corvic blinked and, suddenly, her face was an inch from his. He expected to smell something like a rotting corpse or at least something stale, but no, she smelled like perfume. "But you aren't quite living, are you?"

Corvic quirked an eyebrow. "I'm alive. Look at me. Heartbeat, breathing," he replied with mild indignation.

The woman shook her head. "No, you aren't alive. You don't even know where you are." She turned again and went back to facing the wall. Her resonant moaning resumed.

Corvic climbed back down the ladder, even more confused. He stood there for a moment, trying to figure out what she meant, ignoring the fact that he had just met a ghost. And then, he climbed back up the ladder. "What is this place?"

The woman stopped moaning but didn't turn around. "You'll find out soon enough."

The woman's voice reverberated in his head for hours. Disturbed and restless, Corvic couldn't go back to sleep. So, he dressed and left his room, deciding to wander the Ennervelt Garden. The floorboards creaked with every step, and the entire manor groaned as if swaying like an old clipper vessel in the sea. Most of the doors to the resident's rooms were shut. He descended to the third floor and wandered the hallways. As he meandered aimlessly, he heard noises towards the end of the corridor. They sounded like someone or something breathing heavily. Then a door at the end burst open wide, and a man waddled out of it.

The figure was large, over six feet tall, and very round. His face sat like a sack of potatoes on a beefy neck, and he constantly flushed bright red. His eyes looked swollen shut from his bulbous cheeks. A long, wispy beard grew from a round chin down to his waist. He wore elegant Chinese robes, hemmed in gold, and a little hat on his fat head. In one of his pudgy hands he held a thick, black tome. The colossal man took up the entire width of the hallway.

Corvic was about to turn around and go the other direction, not interested in having another odd encounter, but heard the man shout at him. "You! Come! Kneel before King Yan." As he said this, the man slapped his round belly and it jiggled.

Corvic approached the man and looked up into his portly, red face. "Good morning, sir. I'm Corvic. I'm one of the new staff members. How can I help you?"

King Yan bent at his waist and put his nose close to Corvic's face. The slits in his eyes revealed deep black irises. "Hmmm, a curious one." He straightened up and held the book in front of him. It opened, the spine of it resting in the palm of his hand. The pages moved on their own, flapping erratically until suddenly stopping. King Yan looked down at the text. He muttered to himself in Chinese, by what Corvic could tell.

"Strange one. You exist in two places at once." He snapped the book shut and started a hearty chuckle. "Good luck."

Corvic didn't like the way King Yan wished him luck, but he was becoming used to such weird interactions with the residents. "Thank you," he said, mildly annoyed. Corvic turned around and hastily walked away from King Yan.

He went down to the second floor, skipped it, and went to the first. He didn't want to run into any more residents. It was still another couple of hours before he was expected to be in the kitchen. As he approached the front door to the manor, he spotted Mr. Seker's falcon settled on its perch. Its bright yellow eyes glared at him as Corvic walked outside.

He felt as if he had stepped into a blast chiller. The cold bit his exposed skin. A thick fog hung over the grounds, blanketing the Ennervelt Garden. But as far as Corvic could tell, there was no frost or wind; no snow was falling. Yet, Corvic wondered if he had stepped into the arctic by mistake. He descended the front steps and walked into the cemetery, proceeding slowly so he didn't accidentally trip over headstones.

His fingers caressed the granite and marble markers, tombs, and mausoleums. Graveyards were tranquil. He felt at ease among the dead, much more than he felt among the living. Life seemed somewhat unnatural, a surreal experience. Death would peel back the veil and reveal everything. Only then would he understand the universe's secrets.

Every now and again, he saw the fog move, little swirls as something moved through it just beyond his periphery. A low, guttural growl echoed across the garden. Corvic froze. His eyes darted around, trying to see through the mists. He could see only a few feet in front of him. And then the fog parted, revealing a stocky man with a curly black beard. In one hand, the man carried a golden mace with three lions' heads. The other hand rested on the mane of a large lion, its eyes hungrily staring at Corvic. Sheathed at his hip was a curved scimitar, the hilt adorned with leonine decorations.

"You're brave to walk the Garden before sunrise." The man's voice was smooth and calm.

"I like cemeteries. I visit them regularly," Corvic answered honestly.

"Yes, but none where the dead walk as well." As he spoke, the fog suddenly lifted. All around them were gray forms stalking the graveyard. They hovered over the grass, phased through headstones, trees, and statues.

"Why? Why are they here?" Corvic asked, keeping his voice steady despite the horde of ghosts surrounding him and the lion still growling hungrily.

The man smiled. "Does it matter? The only important question is whether you stay or leave." Every specter in the garden stopped moving and turned their eyes on Corvic.

A cold shiver rippled throughout his body. "I just started. I-I can't just leave."

The man smiled. "So, you stay." The lion next to him growled and slowly stalked forward, lowering itself to the ground, ready to pounce. The spirits closed in around him. As they got closer, Corvic could feel the temperature drop precipitously, crystal frost spread across the ground. The man watched pompously as the ghosts eagerly groped the air, reaching for Corvic's body.

The first of the spirits plunged their icy hands into his chest. They went straight through him, and his entire body convulsed. Then another, and another, until he fell to his knees and was swallowed by the throng of specters. As they stole away the air from his lungs and began dragging his soul from his body, his mind realized this was it: the moment he would die. There was no preventing it, no escaping Death this time. And that realization triggered a panic, unexpected and explosive.

He cried out, begged it to stop, tried fighting against the swarm of ghosts, but his struggle was in vain. He couldn't touch them. So many times before he sought death, yet was always denied. But now, literally in Death's embrace, he wanted to live. He wasn't even sure why. He didn't even know for what he wanted to live. All he knew is he wanted to live. Dying now was ironic ... and cruel.

The assault continued to ravage him, and little by little he felt his soul become untethered from his body, despite how much he willed it to stay. His consciousness slipped away, and the world was dimming to black.

"Release him!" a raspy voice pierced through the hungry groans of the spirits. Immediately, the ghostly mob retreated, leaving Corvic lying semi-unconscious on the frosted grass. Even the man with his lion took a wary step back. Corvic looked around for the source of the voice.

A black-cloaked figure stood near the path. In one skeletal hand it held a large, menacing scythe, which gave off a high-pitched and eerie whistle. The blade was long and curved. The figure's cloak was tattered, ripped and fraying along the hems, with a hood pulled up over the head, shadowing its face. Though concealed from him, Corvic felt an undeniable familiarity with the figure. An overwhelming sense of nostalgia washed over him.

"He isn't yours to claim, Nergal," the high voice whispered malevolently.

The bearded man swallowed. "Yes, of course. Just testing him." Nergal backed up slowly. The lion was now cowed, looking less like a lion and more like a tabby cat. The pair vanished into the wall of fog.

And then the figure's face turned to Corvic. "You want to live?" it asked. Its voice was nothing more than a hoarse whisper, yet it filled Corvic with heavy dread.

Corvic was still trying to get his bearings about him. "Yes," he replied.

"Why now?"

"I don't know."

The figure approached him, gliding across the grass and between headstones. Corvic clambered to his feet, dizzy and nauseous.

"Do you know where you are?" the figure asked.

Corvic wasn't sure, but he guessed anyway. "The afterlife."

The figure started wheezing, which Corvic assumed was a laugh. "Not quite. You aren't dead ... yet."

"Then where am I?"

"You stand at the gate to the afterlife, at the precipice of the dead."

"Why haven't I been here before?" Corvic asked. "I've nearly died several times."

"No, Corvic Mitchell. You've never touched death before. You've stood in cemeteries, dreamed about death, familiarized yourself with it, and even tried to breach the veil. But you have never felt its caress, never seen beyond. Now you have, and so now you know. And now you want to live. Tell me why?"

Corvic shook his head. "I don't know."

The figure was now a foot from Corvic. He could smell its putrid odor, the reek of rotting corpses. "Until you know, you will stay here. You will serve the Chateau Mortem." The figure turned and started to leave.

"Who are you?" Corvic asked. "Who are the residents of Chateau Mortem?"

"You already know."

As the figure walked away, Corvic felt a piece of him being torn away, like his shadow was being severed from his body. Death no longer followed him.

Michael is, and always has been, in love with stories. Even as a lawyer, Michael attempts to merge storytelling with his practice. He has a BA in Creative Writing and is currently working on his first novel. He writes short stories in the meantime while juggling work, family, and the daily rigors of life. He lives in the shade of Mt. Olympus in Salt Lake City, Utah.

https://vocal.media/authors/m-fritz-wunderli

Hell Hound of the Baskervilles by G. Clatworthy

"You can't do this to me."

"It's done, Jones."

"But—"

"Enough! Every agent has a partner. Deal with it."

I stamped my way out of my boss's office. It wasn't professional or mature, but it made me feel better. I slumped into my chair and tapped at the computer screen. I wasn't against people—although what I'd seen of human nature didn't put them in my top ten species—I just couldn't risk exposure. A partner might get too close, and if I shifted in front of them ... then my whole life could disintegrate.

What I needed was a new case to distract me. A ping in my inbox answered my internal plea.

"I could help you turn off the sound on your alert."

I snapped my head up to find the source of the poshest voice I'd ever heard blinking down at me with owlish blue eyes. My gaze wandered up to the huge fluff of hair that sprouted from his round head, giving him a mad professor aura that didn't go with his boyish face.

"Who are you?"

He held out his hand. "Maximillian Baskerville. Everyone calls me Maxi. The boss said to report to you."

I shook his hand. My lips twitched up as he winced at my strength. It was petty, but I gave an extra squeeze before releasing him.

"So, what are your combat skills like?"

He guffawed. I had never heard someone make a sound so accurate for that word before. "Er, not really my forte, what!"

I raised one eyebrow and levelled a stare at him. Things could get ugly in the field when you worked for the Magical Liaison Office and all agents had basic combat training as well as crossbow proficiency—the weapon of choice for our organisation, given it could so easily combine wood and silver in one arrow that would cause most supernaturals to stop in their tracks.

An obvious question rang around my mind, so I spoke it aloud: "Why would they assign me a new partner who doesn't have basic combat training?"

He fidgeted. "Oh, yah, I've been asked to assist; tech support, yah. And ... I've got some knowledge about this case."

I narrowed my eyes at him and turned back to my emails, reading the one marked urgent at the top of my inbox. When I was done, I looked up.

"You have specialist knowledge about an oversized dog that attacked a toff at the Baskerville Hall ... wait." A piece of the puzzle clicked into place. "You're a Baskerville."

"Yah. Ever since the civil war, there have been rumours of a large black dog roaming the estate ... I've done some research, and the boss thought you should have an expert on local legends with you so ... ta-dah! It'll be a jolly lark, what!"

I tuned out his public school boy nonsense. "You ready to go?"

"Er, yah." He pointed to a pristine leather carry all.

I grabbed my handbag and grinned at his puzzled look. My mock crocodile skin handbag didn't look like much, but I'd had it enchanted, and it could hold anything while weighing no more than a regular bag. It contained everything I needed for a mission.

I rooted around inside and withdrew my crossbow to make a point.

Maxi gave a low whistle. "Nice handbag of holding." He held up his fist for me to bump it. I ignored him and led the way to the garage under the London headquarters.

As we took the lift downstairs, I decided to find out more about my new partner.

"Have you got any field experience?" I asked.

He shook his head. "Been here for a year, but no field missions over in tech."

The lift lurched to a halt, and I strode over to my standard issue grey Volvo. I climbed in and programmed the sat nav to take us to Dartmoor. A four-hour drive. I groaned and set off. At least it was mostly motorway and main roads.

As soon as we were outside the horrors of the M25 motorway that ringed London in a multi-laned circle with incomprehensible exit signs, I asked Maxi what he knew about Baskerville Hall and the hellhound.

"Yah, well, it's quite a story. Sir Hugo Baskerville was an occultist at the outset of the civil war. He thought he could tip the balance to favour our side—"

"Which side was your family on?" I asked.

"The royalists." Of course, the posh boy's family were royalists. I kept my eyes on the road as he continued. "So, he started experimenting. According to legend, he managed to open a gate to another realm and a ruddy huge black dog comes through. But, instead of helping, it killed Hugo and set a curse on our family."

"Hang on. He opened a gate to another realm? How did he close it if he was dead? Why didn't more creatures get through?"

"The story goes that his faithful servant stopped the ritual and closed the gate, but he was too late to save his master. Totally sad." His voice lowered into what he must have thought was an approximation of Christopher Lee, but in reality, sounded like he had got a frog in his throat. "Ever since then, the hound has roamed the moors ready to kill anyone who gets in its way."

"Alright, knock the voice on the head," I said. "The file doesn't have any confirmed killings. Sounds like it was a local legend to scare children."

"Oh, it scared the pants off me for sure. I must have been the only child glad to go to boarding school." He shuddered.

I sighed and turned on the radio, tuning it into some cheerful nineties pop music that I bopped along to, tapping the steering wheel with my fingers. Poor little rich brat, sent away to boarding school with his chums, trained up on the classics and how to rule the world. So privileged that he wanted to leave home. Not like me. Forced to live in hiding and then run to survive, I spent my childhood wishing I could have my dad back and looking over my shoulder. Until I could run away and live in plain sight in London.

I shook my head to get away from those thoughts. We weren't going anywhere near my family home in Wales; we were going to rural Devon.

Four and a half hours and one pit stop at a crummy service station later, and we made it to Baskerville Hall. I turned the car through towering stone gates with large dog statues peering down at us as we drove along the gravelled drive. Spears pierced their stony flanks but didn't affect their menacing leers.

Trees lined the drive. Maybe they would give a cheery feel in the summer, but in late autumn with the branches half bare, they looked like they could reach out and touch us through the low hanging mist that clung to the ground.

We rounded a corner, and I stared.

"This is where you grew up?"

"Yah, welcome to the old homestead." He got out of the car and stood looking up at the mansion before us. I gaped up at the huge house before joining Maxi at the foot of the stone steps leading to the huge front door, easily wide enough to fit three people through at the same time. Above the door, a carved black hound glared down at us, a spear through its side as well. Looks like the Baskervilles embraced their gothic past.

The building itself was a red brick mansion with two floors and ten windows spaced neatly along the top floor. More stone dogs watched us from the stone crenelation around its roof. The weak afternoon sun did nothing to dispel the creepiness. A pang of sympathy stuck in my chest; no wonder Maxi was anxious to leave this place. At least I always felt welcome back at home, even if Mum and me had our disagreements.

A howl sounded close by. I unholstered my crossbow and whirled round, aiming in the direction the mounting howls came from. It sounded like there were more than one of the hellish creatures.

Maxi stepped forward just as a pack of six hounds raced around the corner. He disappeared under a mound of dog flesh that yipped and licked at his face. I replaced my crossbow. If these were hellhounds, I was a house cat.

"Just the hunting pack out for an afternoon run. Nothing to worry about!"

I watched Maxi roll around with the dogs. Maybe this was the only affection he'd had growing up. I shook off the sentimentality and headed up the steps to ring the doorbell. It was one of those old-fashioned bell pull contraptions and I yanked it down, hearing the bell reverberate through the hall on the other side of the door.

An elderly gentleman opened the door and stood to one side so we could enter. "We expected you half an hour ago," he sniffed. He wore a black waistcoat over a pressed shirt and grey trousers. I stared for a moment, wondering if I had conjured him; he looked exactly like the butler I expected to answer the door.

"Sorry Watkins. Traffic on the motorway and I needed a bathroom break around Bristol, bladder of a five-year-old, what. Old man in the lounge, is he?" Maxi had shaken off the dogs, and they now followed him, jumping around his feet. One of them sniffed me and I let it lick my hand.

"The study, sir." A flicker of concern passed over the butler's face, but it went so fast that I might have mistaken it.

"Right-o." Maximillian walked into the house and set off down a green carpeted hall, dogs at his heels.

The butler called the hounds to him. "Sir Baskerville doesn't like animals in his study. I will return these dogs to their kennels."

"Right you are," Maxi said, took a deep breath, and entered the study.

I resisted the urge to smooth down my suit jacket as I walked past the weapons on display in the hall. I didn't need to impress anyone. I was the Magical Liaison Office expert here. The panelled door to the study was open, so I strode in without knocking.

An uncomfortable sensation tingled down my skin, making my hairs prick on end. It was powerful magic. I wouldn't put it past the privileged family to have invested in powerful enchantments for a safe. I couldn't pinpoint the source, so I ignored it and took in the scene.

Maxi stood with his head down, staring at his scuffed shoes while an older man sat at a desk that in an ordinary room would have been called oversized. But here, surrounded by walls of bookshelves and enough floor space to fit my entire London flat, it looked like it belonged.

The older man turned the page in a file with deliberate slowness. I knew a power play when I saw it. I strode across the pricey carpet, placed both hands on the desk, and leaned over.

"Are you the owner of the house or the steward?"

The man flushed and looked up. His blue eyes were the same shape as Maxi's, but without the innocent arrogance. He appraised me and smiled.

"You must be the Magical Liaison Office agent. I am Sir William Baskerville, and yes, I own this house and the surrounding lands."

"Er, technically, Grandpa owns it," Maxi piped up. His father gave him a ferocious stare, and he returned to staring at his feet with a mumbled apology.

"In that case, I'd better speak to the real Sir Baskerville."

"That would be Lord Baskerville," Maxi said. I hid the smirk that threatened to cross my face as his father's face reddened.

"He's not well." William regained his composure. "As I believe you know. You are here to investigate the attack on him, after all."

"All the more reason to see him."

Sir William made to stand. I cut him off. "But first, why don't you tell us what you know?"

He sat down again, his mouth tight at my power tactics. "Stories of hell hounds have plagued my family—"

"Maybe because of your choice of décor," I suggested, eyeing the hell hound carved above the fireplace in the study. The stone mason had added rubies for eyes that caught the dim light from the green shaded banker style lamp on the desk.

Sir William gave a small smile, his polite façade back in place. "Perhaps. Regardless, it has always been nothing more than a harmless story told to make children behave. A ghost story to cause chills in superstitious locals on a long winter's evening."

Maxi swallowed hard. Another pang of sympathy washed through me. I could imagine the stories poured in his young ears by his uncaring father.

"But last night ..." He tapped a pen against the desk. "My father was out taking his evening walk—he likes to watch the sun set over the woods—and there was a howl, like nothing I'd ever heard. I dismissed it as a trick of the moors; sometimes the geographical layout causes distortions in light or sound, confusing unwary travellers. But pater didn't come back. I sent out a search party, naturally."

"Naturally." Sending a search party for an elderly man after dark was the least he could do.

"We found him injured. A huge bite mark gouged out of his shoulder. I called for the doctor—"

"Not an ambulance?"

Sir William gave me a look like I had said a dirty word. "My father is not in the best of health; we have a private medical service on call for him. He prefers to be treated at home. The doctor confirmed he was well enough to stay, and we have set up his room to accommodate his wishes."

"OK. But why call the MLO?"

"One of my men saw a creature in the dark. An enormous dog or wolf, larger than he'd ever seen. He claimed it was a hell hound, but we both know there are many kinds of supernaturals and that seems to me a more logical explanation than a mythical dog."

He gave me a half smile and I stiffened. Did he know what I was? How could he tell?

"Right. I want to speak to the witness and your father." I covered my discomfort with curtness.

Sir William nodded. "As you wish." He stood and pressed a brass button on the wall. Seconds later, the elderly butler appeared. "Watkins, take these people to see my father, then Jackson."

"Yes, sir."

We left the room, but Maxi hung back.

I frowned. "Come on Maxi. You're with me."

He gave me a small smile of relief and trailed after me like a puppy I'd rescued from a kicking.

The butler led the way upstairs with surprising speed. Portraits of the Baskerville family lined the stairwell and the hallway. I spotted Maxi's eyes staring back at me from many of his ancestors' pictures. I shivered; it was creepy. I frowned at a darker face painted into the background of a renaissance man with Maxi's frizzy hairstyle—a clear hierarchy between people who looked like him and people who looked like me.

Watkins paused and knocked on one of the identical wooden doors that we passed.

"Come in, what!" barked a voice from the other side.

"Guests to see you, my lord."

"Well, don't keep them waiting. Come in, come in. Don't get many guests nowadays. Maxi! Didn't know you were back from the city. Come in, I said!"

The butler stood by the door as we walked in. My first impression was that Santa had gone on a diet and decided to get some serious bed rest. Most of the old man was covered by a thick, embroidered quilt that looked Victorian, and the rest of him was covered with hair. A bushy white beard sprouted from his cheeks and chin, hanging down to his chest and his head was topped with a mass of hair that stood out in all directions, much like his grandson's, only longer. His eyebrows were determined not to be outdone and bushed up and outwards, so the only parts of his face I could see were a red nose and those Baskerville blue eyes.

Maxi perched on the large double bed and patted the old man's hand as we introduced ourselves.

"Watkins!" Lord Baskerville shouted, making me jump.

"Yes, sir?"

"Didn't see you there. Bring refreshments for our guests. The good kind."

Watkins bowed and left to get whatever the good kind of refreshments were. I shuffled forward, not wanting to be next to the sickbed. It brought back too many memories of my mother's last days. True to his word, the Earl's bedroom had been transformed into a medical centre. A drip connected into one of his stick thin arms and a heart monitor beeped on the other side of the bed.

"Lord Baskerville?"

"Come forward, gel, and speak up. Can't hear as well as I used to, what."

I coughed and tried again. "Lord Baskerville, what can you tell us about the attack?"

"Not much. Sorry to say, not much at all." He shook his head and his beard swung in time with his movements. It was almost hypnotic. "I was taking my evening constitutional. I like to keep these old bones moving—makes it harder for the reaper to catch me, what! There was a howl, so I decided to cut my walk short. Can't be too careful this close to the moors. Next thing I know, I'm on the ground being shaken like I was a chew toy."

"So, you didn't get a good look at it?" I asked.

"'Fraid not, gel. But you're not here to listen to me prattle on. I know why you're really here."

I raised an eyebrow. "You do?"

"The family curse."

Watkins entered the room smoothly, carrying a tray with a teapot, delicate cups, and a plate of the "good refreshments". He set the tray on the edge of the crowded bedside table and poured us each a cup of tea before handing round the biscuits. I took a couple for form's sake, even though sugary snacks didn't really appeal to me. It might have been the lynx side of me, but I preferred a good steak over sweets any day of the week.

The butler coughed and gave Lord Baskerville a meaningful look. "Your son asked me to remind you not to overexert yourself in your delicate state."

The old man guffawed and shifted in his bed, exposing the large white bandage that wrapped around his shoulder. "You can tell my son that he'll have to do more than send visitors up to get rid of me!"

"Very good, sir." Watkins left, and I listened to make sure his padded footsteps disappeared down the hall and didn't stop outside the door.

"The curse?" I prompted.

"Yes! The curse. Pass me one of those Bournevilles, Maxi m'boy. Can't beat 'em, what!" he stuffed the dark chocolate biscuit in his mouth and spoke around the crumbs. "We're cursed."

I waited, but that seemed to be it. "Can you be any more specific?"

"Hmm? No, not really. But everyone round here'll tell you the Baskervilles are cursed. Maxi made a study of it. Caused quite the stir at the local primary school. Got a few letters home about that. Ever since old Hugo—that's the first Earl of Baskerville—decided to raise an army of damned hell hounds and got himself killed, we've been cursed.

"I can see you don't believe me, but we've got the spear that killed the blighter in the armoury. Of course, some say that it escaped and that it haunts the Baskervilles still. Any unexplained death in the family is caused by that hound."

Maxi nodded along. "The last one was Great-Grampy Baskerville. He died from an unknown illness that struck with no warning when he was eighty-six."

"O ... K ... So, no dog bites?"

"Not until me. I think one of the Earls died from a lion bite over in Africa, but no dogs after Hugo."

"Right." I moved on. "But someone saw a dog?"

"Ask Watkins. He fussed around in here so much last night. He was the one who insisted we call your office, even though William hates getting the authorities involved in anything." He yawned.

"Thank you for your time, Lord Baskerville."

"Would you like me to stay with you, Grampy?"

"Just like your mother. But I'll be alright. Feeling a bit tired, anyway. Catch up later, yah." The old man closed his eyes, and we took that as our cue to exit.

Maxi led the way back past the oil paintings until Watkins met us at the bottom of the stairs.

"If you'll follow me, I have Jackson waiting in the kitchen."

A strange whirring made me tilt my head. "Can you hear that?"

The others exchanged glances. Sometimes I forgot how sensitive my hearing was. The whirring got closer as we kept going, and then Maxi tripped over a low robotic vacuum cleaner. It looked out of place in the gothic hall.

"Forgive me, sir. It's meant to come on after dark."

"Can't believe Daddy actually got one. I never thought he'd go for it."

"I believe it was the cost saving that convinced him." Watkins sniffed. "I am fortunate that there is not yet a butler robot."

"No one could replace you, Watkins."

"Let's get a move on," I said. "Jackson's waiting."

We left the Roomba in the main part of the house and stepped through an unassuming door built into a tapestry. On this side of the door, the walls were plain, and the floor was tiled rather than carpeted. Servants' stairs. Watkins showed us down to the kitchen where a tall man paced, worrying his flat cap between his hands. Mud stained the cuffs of his trousers and there was a large, neatly sewn patch above one knee.

"Mr Jackson? I'm Agent Jones and you know Baskerville. Magical Liaison Office. We hear that you saw something last night?"

"That I did, ma'am. Summat right strange."

"Care to elaborate?"

" 'Twas a dog, like none I ever seen before. Huge, the size of a pony and with great slobbering jaws and eyes that shone like coals. The hellhound."

"When did you see it?"

"I was first there, must have been about half hour after sundown. Sir William asked for volunteers for the search party. I knew the Earl's route—see, we often crossed paths when I was searching the woods for poachers and the like. The hellish creature was on him. Gave me chills. I froze to the spot I did before I shouted, and it let go. Must have heard t'others coming cos it ran off then, soon as it saw me."

"Can you show us where this was?"

"Aye."

"Lead on, then."

"Wait, I've got something in the car that can help," Maxi said.

"Just come on, yah." He sprinted off. I shrugged and followed after. Jackson was uncomfortable walking through the main part of the house; his shoulders were tight, and he glanced around in swift bursts like he expected someone to tell him to leave at any minute.

I walked with purpose and hoped it would rub off on him. I considered saying something like, "They're not better than you, they just have money," but that felt condescending, and we needed his help.

At the car, Maxi dug something out of a backpack with a school logo on it. I squinted but couldn't make out what animal it was. Maybe a lion or a pig?

He pulled out a boxy contraption and smiled at us as he extended the silver aerial. "Detection device to pick up magical signatures. This will help us figure out if what we're after is supernatural." He pointed it at Jackson, and the machine stayed silent. "Jackson doesn't give off enough magic for this machine to read, but if I had the bigger version at the lab ..."

He turned it in my direction. I stepped out of the way. "Alright, we get the picture. Let's get a move on before it gets dark." That was close. I didn't need anyone knowing that I was a supernatural. I'd worked hard to keep my true nature a secret, knowing how bad it could get when people found out that a shifter walked among them. Bad was an understatement. Murderous was more accurate.

I clenched my fists as my mind wandered into places that I normally had tamped down so tight I could ignore them. My stride lengthened as my brain whirred. Supernaturals and humans were an uneasy mix. As a lynx shifter, I could pass for human most of the time, and mundanes hated it when you weren't the monster they expected.

I kicked at a clump of grass and looked back. Maxi and Jackson puffed as they tried to keep up with me. Maxi still had that dzraking machine out. I waited halfway up a small hill before telling Jackson to take the lead.

"Not scared are you?" Maxi said with a laugh.

"Scared? I'm not dzraking scared," I lashed out before I could stop myself, hating Maxi's puppy dog eyes.

My mind was still in the past, reliving the last time I saw dad, as the mob took him. I had to spend my life in rural Wales without a dad because humans were too dzraking narrow minded to accept others. And now I protect mundanes from magical beings who actually want to do them harm, knowing that they took away my dad. I forced the grief into anger like I always did. "Let's find this dog."

He bounded on ahead, scanning the path, ignoring my outburst.

"Look here! These readings are off the chart!" Maxi's shout spurred me on to jog the final section.

My muscles responded with ease, and I enjoyed the slight burn from the exercise, but it ended far too quickly.

Maxi spun round and pointed to the screen. A wavy green line spiked across it.

"What does it mean?"

"A strong magical signature was here. My guess is this is what attacked Grampy. Normally any residue is much weaker than this, so, either it came back, or it's something from another realm—one of pure magic. Or ..."

"Or?"

"Or it's hiding close by." He gulped.

I turned in a slow circle, using my enhanced senses to pick out the slightest sound in the trees that surrounded us. The sun hung low on the horizon, a lazy orb finished for the day. The forest loomed on either side, impenetrable to sight. Anything could hide a few feet back and we'd never see it. But my ears picked up nothing. Nothing out of the ordinary: just birds, a small animal scurrying in the undergrowth. I sniffed the air. There was a faint tang of bad eggs.

"What is that smell?"

Maxi gave an exaggerated inhale that made me want to punch him.

I followed the scent and found a huge pawprint pressed into the earth. "Here." Schiztz. This thing was massive. I stretched my hand over the print. My fingers didn't touch the sides.

Maxi got down on all fours and shoved his face into the dirt. "Yah! There is a whiff of brimstone around here, isn't there? Great sense of smell! I'd say this is a clear indication of a creature from another realm. Gah, it's almost as bad as Toffy. He could clear the entire dorm on chilli night!"

A low howl sounded across the moors, interrupting his schoolboy story. It was haunting, with echoes of death singing through the call. My hackles went up, and I snarled. My inner lynx was not happy.

Maxi swallowed.

"It came from the same direction as the house," I said.

"Grampy!" Maxi exclaimed at the same time as I said, "Lord Baskerville."

We ran.

***

My gait was smooth, practised after years of working out in the gym and five mile runs every day, but my lynx longed to break free, knowing I could cover the ground faster in my animal form. I quashed that feeling. I didn't have time to deal with Maxi freaking out at my transformation or anyone at the house mistaking me for the hellhound. Bullet wounds are not fun to recover from.

I pounded on the door, shaking it on its hinges.

Watkins opened the door a fraction of an inch at her frantic banging.

"Let us in!"

"Did you hear it?" His thin voice shook with fear.

I barged past, flinging the door open. "Watkins, we need to barricade the house and I need eyes on the grounds."

"The upper floor, ma'am."

I nodded and took one step towards the stairs when Maxi's father arrived. "What is the meaning of this?"

"You heard the howl?"

"Of course, I did. But you cannot tell me that you believe this balderdash?"

"We found strong magical residue at the attack site and evidence of a large canine. We believe something entered from another realm."

"Another realm? Poppycock!"

"It's true, Papa," Maxi panted from the doorway. "The machine doesn't lie." He waved the black box at his dad and then blinked. He looked like a confused owl.

I stepped back, but Maxi wasn't interested in my magical signature. "Pater, why do you have a magical signature?"

"I'm not magical, you fool," Sir Baskerville sneered.

I believed him. He didn't smell like a supernatural. There was a slim possibility that he was a species I hadn't encountered, but after four years in the London branch of the Magical Liaison

Office, I'd come across pretty much everything the supernatural world had to offer.

Maxi's jaw hung slack, and he stared from his father to the machine then back again.

"Is there another way that your machine could pick up a magical signature from a human?" I asked.

"I suppose if there was sufficient exposure ..."

"Where have you spent a lot of time recently?"

"This is preposterous! I work in my study, tour the grounds, visit my tenants. I haven't been anywhere magical. This whole thing is ridiculous."

The hound bayed again.

I pinched the bridge of my nose and made my decision.

"Right, Maxi, you and I are going to the study with Sir Baskerville. Watkins and Jackson, barricade the downstairs."

I marched to the study and the scrape of furniture rang in my ears as the two humans moved a table in front of the heavy front door.

Inside the study, I almost trod on the stupid robotic vacuum cleaner, and I bent to press its off switch. Close to the floor, the unsettling tingle of magic I had felt the first time I'd entered the room squeezed my chest.

"The readings are stronger here. This is the source, for sure. Oh Papa, what did you do?"

So, Sir Baskerville had played with magic.

"I didn't do anything, you imbecile. I cannot believe the idiocy of my own offspring. I thought some time in the city would do you good, but it's time you came back and started living up to your responsibilities. You are heir—"

Anger built inside me. We didn't have time. My teeth lengthened, and I shoved the old man against one of the bookcases that lined the room.

"Tell us what you did."

His mouth opened and closed in his red face. I loosened the pressure of my forearm against his throat.

"I don't know what you're talking about," he croaked.

I let out a growl of warning. My patience had come to an end.

Something flashed in the corner of my eye. The corner of an occult symbol shone red in the stone floor where I'd scuffed up the carpet ramming Maxi's father into a bookcase.

I released Sir Baskerville.

"You haven't heard the last of this!"

"Shut up!" I said, bending down to pull back more of the carpet.

"I'll ... I'll report you! When I'm through, you'll never work again!"

"Pack it in, pater."

"How dare you!"

Maxi stood and squared up to his father. "Look! Your study is the source of all of this. Do you expect me to believe you didn't summon the creature? That you didn't know?"

"I ... I ... It wasn't me!"

I yanked back more of the double layered carpet with a satisfying rip of the thick material.

Carved symbols and runes covered the stone floor. It looked like dangerous magic, but I wasn't an expert.

"Maxi, how do these symbols work?"

"Fascinating ..." Maxi switched from anger to wonder in an instant. "It looks like they create a gate to another realm but in a separate location ... It's complicated magic, but once it's set up, it can be activated by anyone if they pass over the symbols in the right order ..."

My gaze landed on the innocuous round vacuum cleaner and a thought crystallised. "Does it have to be a living person?"

Maxi tilted his head and ran a hand through his hair, causing it to stick up further. "No, I suppose not ..."

He trailed off as he noticed my gaze.

"You don't think ..."

I nodded. "I think that the Roomba summoned the hellhound."

"Sorry, Papa. I can't believe I thought you might have opened a portal to another dimension." Maxi held his arms out for a hug.

Sir Baskerville looked between us. "You're all bloody mad!" He swept out of the room.

Maxi pulled a face. "Well, Christmas is going to be more awkward this year."

I let out a snort of laughter despite myself. "Right, so how do we reverse this?"

Maxi toed a couple of runes with his shoe. "No idea. This is specific magic. We're probably looking at the original spell the first Earl commissioned to raise the hell-spawn army in the civil war. I could search the records ..."

"Start there."

"What are you going to do?"

"Kill a hellhound. You make sure the gate closes and nothing else gets through."

I left Maxi pulling books off the shelves and hurried back to the others. A glint of metal caught my eye. Weapons. I clambered up a lacquered cabinet that had avoided becoming part of the barricade and grabbed the long spear tipped with black blood that had "Killer of the Hellhound" inscribed on its long shaft.

It stuck fast in its mountings, but after I applied my supernatural strength, it came free. I tested the weight of it. A slight tilt towards the front. But this could tip things in our favour.

A howl came from the back of the house.

I sprinted towards it.

***

Maxi's description of a "ruddy huge black dog" paled in comparison to the beast that stood before us. It was enormous, the size of my car from nose to tail, and it stood as tall as a van. Its coat was coal black with flecks of orange that paid tribute to its hellish roots. Its face was wolf like but with a blunter snout filled with serrated teeth that glinted in the half light of the moon. It glared down at us with eyes that sparked fire as drool dripped from its maw.

I swore.

The creature prowled towards the house, its head close to the ground, sniffing. It sat back on its haunches and howled before leaping at the wall, its clawed feet scrabbling at the brickwork.

I did some mental mapping. It was after the old man.

I made my way to the back door and opened it without a sound. It was set under a staircase to the main house, so I inched forward and used the stairs as cover to assess the situation.

The hellhound flung itself at the wall, shaking the house. Glass shattered under the force of its body.

I gripped the spear, took up a javelin pose I remembered from PE lessons, and launched it at the slavering creature.

My aim was true, but the hellhound's feet slipped on gravel and the spear skimmed its back instead of impaling it. The beast spun round and glared at me.

I whipped my crossbow from its holster and shot it. The small bolt disappeared into its shaggy fur. It growled with pain and crouched.

A shot rang out, deafening my keen ears. Jackson poked a gun out of a downstairs window.

The hellhound leapt with a growl. Jackson pulled at the shutter. He wasn't quick enough. It crunched down with its jaws, shook his limp body like he was a chew toy, and dropped him on the ground.

I sprinted forwards, yelling to get its attention. It turned its glowing eyes on me. I fired off another bolt then ran around the house, leading it away from the civilian.

Hot breath panted behind me as it pursued. It was fast, but its gigantic size made it clumsy. I took the corners tight, staying close to the wall as I completed the lap and ducked into the servants' entrance as it skidded around the corner.

"Jones! There you are!"

"Maxi?" I leaned over my knees, trying to get my breath back.

"Great news! I've disconnected the portal. Nothing else can come through."

I nodded, still out of breath.

"But the curse is real. I found an account. The first Earl tried to bring over a demon. He wasn't strong enough to bind it to him, and the demon sent through a hellhound to kill the Earl. Before he died, the Earl shut the gate and banished the demon, but the demon vowed that if they ever reopened the portal, it would hunt down the Baskerville heirs."

I stared at him. This was a lot of information to take in while a huge hellhound sniffed outside.

"It won't stop until it's killed Grampy, then Papa, then me."

"Good work," I managed to say. "You stay here. I'll deal with the dog."

I checked my crossbow and gathered up all my bolts into my handbag.

"How will you stop it?" Maxi asked.

"They killed it with a spear a couple of hundred years ago. I just need a clear shot." I didn't tell him that I had a few supernatural skills that would help too.

"Be safe."

I nodded and headed for the door.

***

The hellhound had given up on chasing me and was back to snarling at the upper windows of Baskerville Hall. A shout sounded from inside. Someone threw a vase from an open window.

"Not the Ming!" came Sir Baskerville's voice as the priceless porcelain shattered against the hellhound's thick skull.

"Gotcha! Attaboy. Now what else have we got?" Maxi's grandfather threw another vase out of the window.

I shook my head. Someone was going to get hurt. And if I had anything to do with it, it would be the hellhound.

I left my hiding place under the stairs, prepped my bolts, and fired as fast as I could. Bolt after bolt thudded into the creature's side. It growled, a low rumble that shook the ground and it turned back to me.

I squared my feet, ready to dodge its attack, and reloaded my crossbow. Just one shot in its fiery eyes should do it. I aimed.

The hellhound dipped its head, bared its teeth, and charged.

"I've come to help—"

Maxi appeared at the doorway. I motioned for him to get back and turned my attention back to the beast. This was my chance.

I loosed off the bolt. It sank deep into the creature's eye but didn't stop it. I jumped to the side. Too slow. It caught me with the edge of its muzzle, dagger sharp teeth grazing my side.

I crashed to the ground, crossbow raised.

Behind the hellhound, Maxi gaped.

I rolled, avoiding snapping teeth and getting in a kick against the hell hound's wet nose. As it lifted its head in anger and pain, I saw Maxi sidling up to the discarded spear by the house.

"Maxi! No!"

He hefted the spear and threw it. His aim was poor, but the hell hound was a big target, and the tip bit into its flank.

It yelped in pain and spun, its fiery eyes focused on Maxi. I pushed myself up and sprinted towards it. Too late. It swatted him to one side with a huge paw and he lay still on the ground.

Enough.

With a scream of frustration, I shifted into my lynx form, my clothes disappearing into the magic. I leapt at the enormous dog, sinking my claws into its black hide. It growled and whipped round, shaking me from its back.

I flipped in the air and landed on my feet. Thank you cat reflexes. I hissed at the creature. We circled each other, waiting for a gap.

I feinted to the side. It pounced, jaws open and sulphuric breath filling the air. I dived in the other direction, used the wall as a springboard and ended up on its back again.

This time, I dug my claws in, raking along its side. Hot blood covered my feet. It yowled and spun in a circle, snapping at me.

I curled my short tail up and sank low against its greasy fur as I clung on. It couldn't get me.

It snarled in frustration and fell to the ground. I leapt to avoid being crushed as it rolled on its back. One of my legs caught under its enormous body and I let out a shriek of pain as bone crunched. I pulled myself free.

My leg burned with pain. I put it on the ground and the pain ramped up from burning to blazing. Time to end this.

Using my uninjured legs, I launched myself at its exposed belly, scratching deep gashes into its speckled skin. It squirmed under me and tried to right itself. I moved forward and bit down on its neck. Warm blood hissed into my mouth tasting of sulphur. My stomach roiled in disgust, but I clung on as it twisted and finally got back onto its feet.

I dangled from its neck, refusing to let go as its life blood poured over me. It snarled and took a shaky step forward before it collapsed to the ground. I hung on for a few more seconds as the flow of blood stalled, then released my jaws.

Instinct took over, and I retched out the blood that I'd swallowed along with the rest of my stomach contents. After I was finished, I shifted back into my human form and limped over to Maxi's prone body.

I looked down at Maxi, sprawled on the floor. He had risked his life for me, and I had done nothing to deserve it. I had written him off as a useless rich boy and he'd saved my life. He was a better person than I was.

I sat on the ground, damp seeping into my suit trousers, and cradled his head. Rummaging in my handbag, I found a bottle of Cure All and uncorked it. The herbal spell of aniseed mixed with alcohol stung my nostrils. I dripped it into his mouth until he spluttered.

"That is awful. Reminds me of this time in France when we had a bad bottle of vino ..."

I smiled as he rambled on about his adventures and took my own swig of the disgusting liquid. He would be fine.

***

A week later, I strode into my boss's office. I had given this a lot of thought.

"Jones?"

"I want a new partner."

He leaned back on his desk and considered me. "Really? Just the other week you wanted to work alone."

I shrugged. "Things change."

"Alright." He clicked his mouse a couple of times. "It looks like there's a couple of agents available ..."

"I want Maxi."

"The tech guy?"

I nodded. He had laid down his life for me. He might be annoying and green as a grasshopper, but I could trust him.

My boss frowned. "He'll have to pass basic training …"

"He will." I would coach him.

"OK then, you have yourself a partner."

G Clatworthy started writing during the 2020 lockdown (her first book was called *The Girl Who Lost Her Listening Ears*, which tells you all you need to know about lockdown!). She soon switched to fantasy, and she loves mixing the magical with the mundane, especially if it involves dragons! She lives in Wiltshire, UK with her family and two cats. When she's not writing, she enjoys playing board games, drinking tea and eating chocolate.

Note: this story is in UK English.

https://www.gemmaclatworthy.com

Yours Truly by Isa Ottoni

Eerie Publisher House, Lundin

Mr Brian Sage, Editor

November 22nd, 1902

My dearest friend,

You are probably wondering where the rest of this correspondence is, likely urging your assistant to look for the pages I owe you, the final draft of the interview that would make our careers—mine as the first journalist to have ever interviewed a Fairy, and yours as the brilliant publisher who was brave enough to grant me this chance. But within this light, wrinkled envelope, you will find no such thing. The papers have not been lost in the railway lines, nor has the postal coach misplaced them. You needn't yell at your assistant; the boy's nerves shall be spared. The lack of weight to this correspondence is entirely my fault.

You believed in me, and I failed you. All those days we spent preparing for this—the research, the drafts, the hopes and dreams we shared in the darkest hours of night, while indulging with your most expensive brandy—were but for naught. Although I have managed to find and indeed speak to the fairy—and will recount what I heard and saw—I fear we won't be able to publish it. I do not wish to risk you, my dear friend, being ridiculed for my incompetence. My hope is that, as I narrate the mishaps of my journey, you will come to understand.

However, I should also warn you that I do have an ulterior motive for writing to you today. There is something I must tell you, something I have discovered and that is, perhaps, even more valuable—or at least that is my hope. I won't know until my return. But I beg that you endure my clumsy ramblings before I can manage the words out and onto this parchment.

I do hope you understand.

It took me weeks to locate the brook of trees marked on the map. I travelled from village to village, collecting stories from innkeepers, bakers, blacksmiths, butchers, maids, until I finally found the path into Fae: a narrow stone lane between an Ash tree and a Blackthorn at the top of an ancient barrow in the country. I was very lonely walking the enchanted trails of the woods, with only the trees and the flowers and the knowledge that you were waiting eagerly for my return keeping me company. When thirsty, I found a bubbling brook which got me on the right track. Then I sat by the waterfall and waited.

I don't know what I had expected, but surely it was not what I found. As dusk fell over the forest, casting the sky in purple light, the fairy approached me with suspicion. I held my breath under their scrutiny. Skin as black as the midnight sky, eyes as bright as the most radiant star. The fairy was tall—not like the pixies drawings we had dug up in that old library—and watched me through slit pupils, like a snake. He wore a frock coat and a cravat, and I felt quite inadequate in my light lounge suit. His dark indigo vest reminded me of the one you wore when we said our goodbyes. I could go on, his appearance was rather striking, but suffice to say he dressed as fashionable as us gentlemen would dress at the Queen's Yule Ball—that is if I, a modest journalist(!) were ever invited. But upon further observation, I noticed the garments were not made of fabric or wool, but were woven from leaves, and twigs, and flowers, and precious gemstones. He greeted me in a language I did not understand.

I introduced myself nevertheless and disclaimed my intentions. His thin lips parted in a snarl, pointy teeth bared. I feared for my life then—feared never seeing you again—but as you wisely advised me before, I quickly offered him a trinket, a gold teaspoon, as a gift and token of my good intentions.

Good morrow, he said upon accepting the present, his accent foreign but clear to my frightened ears.

Master Lore was his name, and he agreed to answer the questions you and I had prepared together: what his occupation was, where he lived, what was magic like to him, where his wings were (for I could not see the set). But for each question, I got a slightly different response, and never the one I was hoping for. Even though his grammar was perfect by all standards—even yours, the best editor of the kingdom; the man behind the first and most successful occultism bulletin—his answers barely made sense. You will see what I mean.

He said his occupation was fairying, a full-time position he did with pride. What did he mean by fairying? He meant being, and breathing, and living. What about those deals we so often hear about? Could he offer me the world in exchange for something as trivial as my soul? What would he do with my soul? he asked, and then offered me his instead. Did he have a soul at all? He couldn't recall, but if so, he had no use for one. He would very much like another trinket though.

Lore lived in that very forest, under the bubbling brook I had stopped earlier for a drink. Was it damp and cold and lonely? Yes, he said, the loveliest place indeed. His family often visited; they had parties that lasted centuries under the starry endless night. Centuries? I gasped. Oh yes, indeed, he assured me, he and I had been talking for years already, as time slips by fast when one is having fun. I shuddered then, dreading that I might find you, my dear friend, an old man upon my return. I know now that is not the case. I came back to the Inn but a week after my departure. Master Lore seemed to have a different understanding of time than we do.

To my astonishment, the word "magic" was foreign to him. His tongue stumbled over the syllables, drawing giggles from his throat—giggles that sounded eerily like bells. What did magic mean? I told him about the spells, the rituals, the potions, the abracadabra incantations we so often see in tales of his kind. He still didn't understand. I breathe, he said, and the realm breathes with me. That was the most coherent sentence he could manage about the topic.

What about his wings? Wasn't he supposed to have them? Birds had wings, he said, and he was not a bird. Insects had wings too, he continued, and bats and sometimes fish. He was none of that. What was he, then? His answer was simple: Well, I am, of course! Did he fly? Yes, he said, always; I am flying right now. He was not, as his bare feet were rooted on the grainy ground, but he didn't seem to grasp the difference.

You can imagine my frustration, dear friend. Speaking to him was like speaking to a mad butterfly, and not realising the one mad was me for speaking to a foolish bug. He seemed to enjoy my grievance, noting how beautiful my cheeks and ears had become with all that red smeared over them.

I offered him another trinket, a porcelain doll which belonged to my late mother.

Please tell me about yourself, I finally pleaded, and let him speak freely. He relished the sound of his voice, and I did my very best to follow the winding paths his story took.

He was Master Lore, but that was not his real name. He kept his name in a locked box, lest someone steal it. Lore was a name given by one of our kind, a pretty thing he had for dinner one night, who tasted of apples and heartache. I kept my face straight as he laughed upon remembering he had indeed struck a deal with the little thing—a kiss in exchange for a secret. He could not remember what the secret was, but she left with his kiss and a wholesome heart. I breathed out, relieved that the girl had survived this eerie encounter, but now that I think about it, I am not entirely sure. Did I misinterpret his story?

Was he in fact saying he ate the poor little thing? Perhaps he had her over for dinner, but what did he mean about her tasting like heartache? Alas, I guess I will never know.

His family enjoyed bathing in the sun, he went on, fancied stretching their branches towards the heavens, dancing with the wind, and also running along the shore, wetting the grounds and playing inside animals' stomachs. They were wicked things, he promised, filled with mischief and murk. He much preferred the umbra, collected them into his skin.

That was when he asked me a question. Why had I summoned him there? I told him about our project, my life's work! I told him about our deadline and about you, dear friend. I said you would be waiting for my return.

He asked then if I loved you. The question caught me entirely off guard. What did he know about love? He said he knew it all. Ignoring all my following questions, he played with the trinkets I had offered. The interview would be over, I understood, unless I answered his question truthfully.

We have now reached the part where I tell you what I promised I would. What I hinted at in this letter, what I have struggled to keep hidden inside my heart.

The part where I tell you that I said yes, indeed, I loved you.

Please forgive me if my words bring you sorrow, but I love you, dear friend. I have loved you for a while now, though I cannot say precisely when these feelings began afflicting my troubled heart. But I do. I love you.

He asked if I had ever told you that, and I said no, indeed I hadn't. He asked why. I didn't know why.

Was it because I was afraid, because I feared your rejection? Am I the coward I have always believed I was not? Indeed, I think I am.

As I write to you, my dear, dear friend, I consider throwing this letter in the fire, setting this clumsy declaration ablaze, and scribbling an awkward excuse about how I failed to locate the fairy, how I failed you.

But Lore's words upon our departure still burn in my mind and chest—what is the point of love if one is doomed to love alone?

And that is why instead of a manuscript, an interview that would set our careers into a shooting success, you are receiving this ... love letter. I won't burn it. I won't rewrite it. I will fold this wrinkled piece of parchment and have the boy that serves this Inn send it back to you.

I hope you won't hate me for disclosing my affection, but I will understand if you do. I have but a penny to my name and nothing to offer you but my heart. I hope that is enough.

I shall arrive in a month, perhaps shortly after this letter reaches you, perhaps without giving you enough time to make up your mind about me. But I won't come to you. I shall wait for you instead, at the park, on the winter solstice day at noon. If you choose to come, you will find me below the Rowan tree, where we had that pleasant picnic lunch and came up with the idea for this never-to-be interview.

You needn't come, but I shall wait for you, nevertheless.

Yours truly,

Oliver Quill

Isa Ottoni (she/her) writes fiction with a spark of magic and fantasy with a spark of reality. When Isa is not writing, she is teaching and putting her PhD in food consumption sciences to good use, even though she would much rather be writing or reading about — you guessed, magic. She believes fantasy is what makes life fun, and that is a hill she is ready to die on. Isa was born and raised in Brazil but moved to Portugal seeking a new adventure. She lives with her incredibly supportive husband and their dog, a mischievous little mutt who thinks himself the king of everything that light touches. Isa doesn't have the heart to contradict him.

https://isaottoniwrites.wixsite.com/website

Section 4:
Society
VS
Humankind

The Act of Never Fitting In by MJ James

Most Travils do not stay with their birthing unit until they are bestowed. More than half are given up at birth, handed directly to the Nit nurses who clean them, feed them, and wait for a Travil to pick them up. Some children last a few years in the home until the Nit and Ou children's demands become overwhelming. Then the Ou decides it is time for their Travil child to head off to the school full time.

The Ous and Nits remember them in offhanded comments when asked how many children they have produced. "I had two Travil children," they may say. "When we had our Nit child, the oldest Travil moved to the school. Then we had a pair of Ous and another Travil that went to the school after birth."

Only the Travil parents remembered Travil children. They are allowed in the Travil school at any time. They randomly sit in on lessons when their other children do not need them. They even bring their Travil children back to their birthing house if the Nits and Ous went on vacation without their Travil unit. It is essential for the Travil parent to bond with their Travil children; after all, the Travil parent will help their Travil children with their own births.

I was the oldest child in my birthing unit. Until I was three, I would spend the day with my Nit as she tried to start her store or have my Ou carry me through town, high on his shoulders. They dressed me in the Nit's one-piece pantsuit I preferred and allowed me to keep my hair short. I was young and their only child, so the pampering was overlooked.

After I turned three, I was required to attend four hours of nursery training each day. My Travil would force me to wear the long open dresses required of all Travil. I also had to grow my hair. I was brought to the school and put in a room full of other Travil children and many dolls. The children would pick up their favorite dolls and change their diapers and clothes during the entire play session. They would take their dolls on playdates with other Travil children's dolls. They would put them down for naps in the play beds or put their doll under their shirt and pretend to be carrying the child for their birthing unit.

The children would argue about how many children they would birth. After proudly proclaiming that they would have a hundred bazillion zillion, they would turn and ask me how many I would have.

"No, thank you," I responded.

One day, Netli, a Travil with curly red hair already hanging down to their lower back, insisted that I must have children. I walked away and picked up two dolls, trying to see what the other children saw in them. Netli found me and insisted again. I picked up the dolls and threw them across the room. All the children in the room burst into tears when the doll's ceramic heads smashed into pieces.

When my Travil came to pick me up, the instructors, all elderly Travil past their child-bearing years and already having helped with their grandchildren, begged my Travil parent to have me board at the school.

My Travil was nearly due with the birthing unit's second child, so when they declined, the elderly Travils didn't push too hard. They assumed I would be in their care full-time after the child was born.

Less than a month later, the mandatory nursery class had ended, and my Travil was not waiting for me. My teachers put me in line with the other Travil children. We marched to the dining hall, where we sat on long benches and ate the food given to us. There were no extra treats or funny stories. We sat in quiet. After the Travil nurses took our plates, they led us to the entertainment room where a cartoon Travil taught the Travil children about the adventure of raising children.

While the children laughed and clapped, I went into the corner of the room and cried.

I was being forced into the school's scratchy pajamas when one of the Travil teachers came and retrieved me. My Nit was standing at the front of the school. She had come to tell me all about the birth of my Travil sibling and bring me home.

At six, I started attending training full-time. My Travil parent would place my Travil sibling in their shoulder wrap and march me up to the school with a handful of other Travil parents and children.

At school, the other children teased me constantly. I was the only non-boarded child with a sibling. I never once complained, too afraid that my birthing unit would decide it would be better to move into the school. I was seven years old when I noticed the signs of pregnancy in my Travil, all learned from my early class education.

My sibling started nursery school.

My Nit had finally opened her store.

My Ou was promoted to lead builder.

Even I understood that three children would be a lot for my Travil unit.

I tried to help out as best I could. I started reviewing the accounting books my Nit brought home from the store. At first, the numbers did not make sense, but I borrowed some of her books and taught myself what I could. Once I could balance her books, I began to sneak in and read over my Ou's project expenditures. They were not all that much different. I found myself writing him notes, guiding him on how best to proceed with his project's finances. I then snuck my Ous books and taught myself the basics of building. I began to leave notes for him on the best way to run his project. My logic seemed sound to my seven-year-old self. If I helped them with their job, they would have more time to help the Travil with the babies.

Eventually, my Nit began to leave the store information on her desk when she came home. I would grab everything and take it into the closet of the room I shared with my Travil sibling. I would balance her books and make recommendations for orders. I would find other sheets hidden in the pages, ones with logic or random math problems. I would do these also, in case they were important. At times, there would be books in the stack. Some books taught math and science that I did not return for a few days. Other books were about people who never lived. Those I would stay up all night reading.

I was not quite eight when the new child was born, an Ou. I was the last child my age who was not a boarder at my school. I cried the night he was born and all the next day at school. I tried to prepare myself for the benches and lousy entertainment. I tried to picture myself learning about children and pregnancy and keeping house for the rest of my days. I tried not to think about the math and science books. I tried not to think about the stories. I would have to be happy with my school's books, which showed Nit, Ou, and Travil anatomy. The ones who told the story of the happy Travil who grew up in school and were then bestowed to a matted couple they had never met and went on to have a dozen children. All the time, they smiled, delighted with their life.

But when the bell ended, my Nit was there to pick my sibling and me up, much to the school's disappointment.

That night, it was my Travil sibling's turn to cry and cry. They thought they would finally be allowed to live in the school with all their friends. The next day, my sibling stayed at school, but my Travil brought me home.

There were three more children. One Nit child when I was nine years old. One more Ou child when I was eleven years old. Lastly, one more Travil child when I was twelve years old.

When I turned 16, I was in my last year of schooling. Students were already being selected for bestowal. I stopped combing my hair or washing my face. I put on dresses that were not washed. When the mated pairs came to choose their Travil, they would turn away from me in disgust. The teachers called my birthing unit to complain about my hygiene. The teachers gave me demerit after demerit. My behavior continued.

At the end of the year, more than half of my peers had been bestowed. Those who had not been picked stayed to help at the school until they were selected. Much to the dismay of the entire community, I stayed home.

The first day after graduation, my Nit brought me to her store. I helped stock shelves and worked on inventory. I dusted and cleaned the window, picking up a vase with a single purple glass Turpan flower. It seemed out of place on the otherwise empty window seal. The store stayed empty. The next day and the day after, I stayed in the back room of the store. I worked on books and inventory, much like I had done for years. Gradually, the shoppers returned to the store, happy to pretend I was not there.

A month later, my Nit handed me a list and asked me to go to a supply store. When I walked across the main town center, the security Ous scowled at me. The Nits avoided me. The Travil held onto their children and loudly told them what an abomination I was. I don't know who threw the pebbles. I just felt one strike my side, then another. I kept walking, afraid, but more afraid to show my fear. The stones stopped hitting me as I neared the store. I reached to open the door, but before

I could grasp the handle, it opened seemingly independently. The shopkeeper appeared and stood in front of the door. She did not say anything and did not move. I held my head low, ensuring my eyes were trained on the ground. Then I held up the note, not too close to her face. "My Nit asked me to help our household," I mumbled.

The shopkeeper dressed in the traditional one-piece suit, the coloring bright orange like the sun. It was an extravagant choice for a Nit to wear. Nits were given some leeway in their outfit's hue, but most chose to stay with the more traditional dark coloring. Travil were required to wear only white or cream-colored skirts draping right above our ankles. While I waited, I imagined walking around in such bright clothing. I imagined owning my own store and having the right to deny someone to enter. I waited unmoving until the Nit grabbed my list, ripped it in half, and placed it back in my outreached finger. I mumbled thanks and headed back to my Nit's store. I could feel everyone in the square staring at me, but I was grateful that no one struck or spoke to me.

When I arrived at my Nit's store, I handed her the ripped note and returned to the back room. I tried to focus on the ordering. When I couldn't, I tried to read my current math book. My mind kept returning to the feel of the pebbles hitting me, the jeers of the Ous, and the judgment of the Travil. My hands wouldn't stop shaking, and my breath was rapid. I tried to calm myself down, but I mostly wished I could be normal.

My Nit did not speak of the incident at our evening meal. I retired to my room, as was my custom. Except instead of studying, I went straight to bed, hoping to get this day over with.

The next day, I went back to work with my Nit. I was happy to return to my routine until my Nit walked up to my desk, holding another list. I hurriedly moved the advanced building text, hoping she had yet to see it. She waited for me to take the list and stand up. As I moved to the door, she followed. She paused long enough to lock her door and then walked beside me. I followed the same path as the day before, although there were no pebbles or mocking this time. Instead, everyone stopped and watched us move on our way.

When we reached the shop, the same shopkeeper stood before her door. She wore a rich purple outfit, nearly as bright as her clothes from the day before. When I paused, my Nit kept walking. She raised her hand to her forehead in the traditional Nit greeting and started speaking.

"Good Midday to you, Takil. I hope that your children are well."

"They are. My children are with their Travil unit at the moment." At this, the Nit glanced at me.

"Have you met my child, Takil? They have not been selected for bestowal yet. Until they are selected, they are attending to my store running errands for the household, as is the responsibility of Travil without children to care for."

Even I knew that this was stretching the role of a Travil. Travil who were allowed to run errands were usually old, or at least past childbearing age.

"It is not proper," Takil said.

"The situation is unique, but I would not dishonor my child by refusing to allow them to help the household."

"They should be up at the school."

"It is the tradition for our Travil children to board there, but it is not required. As you know, my child was not exceptionally skilled at childbearing as a Travil should be. We are concerned that they will never be selected and decided to keep them home."

"I heard they were the first Travil in three generations to cause harm to their training child, and I remember the incident with the doll."

"Exactly. Would you and your mate have picked them for your bonding unit?"

"We most certainly would not."

"That is our concern also. Yet, having no role in the community would not be productive for our child. So, we decided to keep them in our household to help out. As you know, our Travil had two other Travil children. They are busy at the school with our youngest and helping the middle Travil child with their new family. Having our eldest to help with household needs is beneficial."

I stood to the side with my head lowered. I did not move through the conversation, but I heard every word. I found myself being both grateful for my Nit advocating for me to have a role that did not involve children and ashamed at the burden that I must be to my family. To show any deviation from a traditional Travil part would mean my death and the death of those involved. Yet, as my Nit had so aptly put, I was the worst Travil in generations. In my heart, I knew that I was not a Travil. Yet I wasn't a Nit or an Ou either. I was something else, something outside our system. I couldn't help the shame that if my Nit knew, she would be handing me off to the security Ous, not advocating for me to have a place as a Travil.

Takil finally took the list from my outstretched hand.

"I cannot speak for every shopkeeper. However, they may do as the other Travils. They must come in the side entrance, never the front, and will wait quietly for me to finish with my customers. Then I will help them. Everyone must have a role, but I don't much appreciate that their role has to infringe on my business."

"Of course, Takil. We completely understand." Then my Nit turned and walked around to the side entrance. I turned and tried to hurry after her. We watched Takil return to her store and help the one customer in there. She made a point of taking an extremely long time talking to her.

"I think you have this now," my Nit said. Then she turned and walked out of the store.

I waited nearly a quarter day before Takil finally put the items and the invoice in my hand. Since then, it had gotten faster. The shopkeepers always made me wait as long as possible, but they were busy and eventually sent me back to our shop. Little did they know that I was also the one that paid them. The ones that served me faster, I paid quickly. Those who made me wait all day were only paid once I could no longer hold off. Ultimately, it meant nothing, but I still did it.

After the second visit with Takil, my Ou instructed me to follow him before our evening meal. He let me into the basement, his private space. He showed me the exercise equipment and how to use it. He taught me how to defend myself if someone tried to hurt me. I practiced with him for a time, and then he handed me a key to the room. I continued to train on my own.

The days continued. My siblings left the house. The oldest Ou was working with our Ou as a low-level builder. He had a bonding unit with a Nit and Travil child. He had sent the Travil child to the school straight after birth, a point he told my bonding unit loudly whenever he visited. My Nit sibling was mated but was holding off on a bonding unit to focus on work and each other. My youngest Ou sibling was unmated and was working on an advanced degree. He did not visit often, but when he did, he always left behind the textbooks of courses he finished. Occasionally, I would see my Travil siblings around the town. They both refused to acknowledge that we were related. The oldest had nine children, and the youngest had birthed three already.

I had seen 27 years and was the oldest unbestowed Travil in our town's history. I was happy with my life. I ran errands and kept my Nit's store. At home, I tried to help around the house, although often, I caused more problems than helped. I was happy. I thought I was safe.

Perhaps I became too accepted. Maybe that is why the mated Nit and Ou walked into our household and informed our birthing unit that I would be their Travil. They came during the evening meal. I saw them invited in, curious why they would be at our house. Then I heard their claim. I listened to my Ou try to dissuade them. They were outraged, rightfully so. It was their choice, and my Ou had no right to question their decision. I had no right to question their decision. Still, I appreciated my Ou trying.

After the bonded pair left our house, I excused myself and went to my room. I tried to keep my crying quiet, hoping my birthing unit would mistake my actions for joy.

Tomorrow, I would be bestowed. I would join a pair mated for over fifteen years before they decided to have offspring. I would be their third, required to join the Nit's egg and the Ou's sperm and grow a child within me. Then, I would be required to do it again as often as they wished. I would be required to care for the offspring.

My purpose in life has always been to care for offspring. I had been told that since I was very young, but it never felt like a happy thing to me. Yet, if I refused, I would die.

No Travil refused. It is our purpose. My classmates had looked to this point joyfully, imagining all they would do for their offspring.

I just wanted to cry. When the tears had dried up, I sat wondering if maybe death was preferred. I wouldn't wait for the security Ous to sentence me. I would do it on my own.

There was a knock at my door. My Nit entered. She thankfully did not appear to notice my face puffed up from crying.

"There is time," she said. "Let's spend the morning at the store."

I was surprised that the sun had risen, and I had spent the entire night crying. I put on a fresh Travil outfit. My Nit stayed in the room with me. Not many Nits and Ous saw their Travil children on their bestowal day.

I checked my face in the mirror to make sure that others could not tell I had been crying. My Nit looked up at me, and for the first time, I realized we were not much different. We both had slender builds. My chest was slightly larger but had always been small for a Travil. My hair hung down to my waist, as was customary for a Travil. My Nit's hair was cut to her shoulders, as was expected.

I spent the morning at the store creating a year-long plan for my Nit. It was a template she could follow. My greatest hope was that the store would survive. I laid out variations for different situations trying to make it as flexible and easy to follow as possible. It would not cover everything, but maybe it would be enough.

I was finished by the time that midday hit. My Nit closed the store, and I said goodbye. No matter what happened next, I would never be seeing the store again.

When we reached our dwelling, I walked to my room to change. There were two outfits laid out on my bed. One was a traditional bestowal gown. The other was one of my Nit's outfits. I walked up to it and tentatively reached down to grab it. I held it up, examining it. It was different from the flowing material that I was required to wear. It was a tight one-piece suit with material that clung to each leg. It was made to complement Nits' flat build, to accentuate the slenderness of both shoulders and hips. The material was strong and flexible, to move with the Nit as they did whatever procedural role they had chosen.

I held the outfit in front of my body and examined myself in the mirror. My chest would show, but my build was not far off. I lacked the hips necessary for a Travil to birth lots of healthy children.

There was movement behind me in the mirror, and I looked to see my Ou standing in my doorway. I dropped my Nit's clothing and backed away.

"The choice is yours," he said. "We will help you the best we can, either way."

It was then that I realized that my life was not a secret, at least not in this dwelling. My birthing unit had known and supported me the best that they could. I stood frozen, reliving my life with this knowledge. It was apparent that they knew and that we all had just pretended too afraid to address how different I was. I had always felt an abnormally strong connection to my birthing unit, but standing there, I knew how lucky I was. I realized how much I was going to lose. No matter what I chose, I would have to leave them and the safety they had given me.

I picked back up my Nit's outfit.

He nodded, no hint of surprise on his face. Then he handed me a band of tight material.

"Put this under. It will help."

I took the material and held it, uncertain. I looked at my Ou and saw his embarrassment. It was then I understood. It was to help flatten my chest, the area of my body reserved for my children. I nodded my understanding.

He leaned over and placed a kiss on my cheek, an unheard-of expression of devotion for a Travil child, then he turned around and left me.

I dressed. The material flattened my chest and made it difficult to breathe, but it worked. I was not completely flat, and my hips were not completely straight, but looking in the mirror, I did not recognize who was looking back at me. I was no longer a Travil. I was me, or at least as close as I had ever been.

My hand reached for the hair flowing down my back. Only Travil wore their hair long. It was not practical for the long strands to hang down and get in the way while a Nit or Ou was productive.

I had always hated my hair, and the thought of it going filled me with unexpected joy. I looked around for something sharp. I moved to the grooming area that I shared with my Travil. Of course, there was nothing. I turned to leave and found my Travil entering the room with a pair of scissors in their hand.

I watched them, uncertain of how they would feel. I was their child, one of the three that they could keep past adulthood, and I was now dressed as a Nit. I was turning away from everything that they loved, all the hopes and ambitions they had. I felt sad, and then I felt even more miserable when I realized that I would not make a different decision. I could not. I had never been a Travil.

They didn't speak. They motioned me to turn around so that my back faced them. Then they picked up the scissors and cut off my silky brown hair. In less than a minute, my hair was gone, clipped clear up to my shoulders.

They used their hands to turn me around, and I saw that they were holding back tears. My Travil gathered me in their arms and held on tight.

"I'm sorry," I whispered.

"All I have ever wanted was you to be safe," they said. Then my Travil turned around and left me.

There was not much time before the mated pair would arrive. I needed to leave.

I went back to my room, uncertain about what to bring or where to go. When I entered, I found my Nit sitting on my bed.

"It won't be easy," she said. "If we could keep you here, we would, but it is no longer safe for you."

"How long have you known?" I asked.

"We have always known," she said. "We have been preparing for this day for a long time. We have been hoping that it never had to happen. There are others like you, others who are born one way but are truly another. They have been guiding us since we found them when you were in the early grades. They told us to keep you here as long as we could, that it would be safer for you. We knew it was hard for you having to pretend, but we made it as easy as we could. But now you must go."

She stood and handed me a pin. It was a purple Turpan flower, a flower so rare that it was said to be priceless. The same flower that stood on the windowsill of the shop.

"Travel to Erriwald. Put on the pin and order a meal. Someone will help you. If no one shows, get a room and try again the next day. If no one shows in three days, leave and go somewhere else. Try to start a new life on your own. There are new papers in the bag. Keep looking for the symbol. That is how you will find others. Be careful and be discreet."

I looked at the pin. My birthing unit had not just been helping me. They had put themselves out to help others like me. I wondered how many people had entered the shop because of the flower. I wished they had told me sooner. I wish I had known that I was not alone. I had so many questions, but there was no longer time to ask. There was a knock at the front door.

My Nit put her hands on my shoulders. Tears were falling freely down her face. I felt myself starting to cry and tried to stop. If I lost control now, I would never be able to finish. She handed me a bag and walked away.

"We will distract them, but you won't have long. Slip out the window and don't be seen."

Then she was gone, and I was all alone.

I put the pack on my back and quietly opened my window. I lived on the bottom floor of the house, so it was not a long drop. When my feet hit the ground, I heard voices. They were coming to my room. They were pretending to present me to them. I did not even take the time to shut the window. I began to run then thought better of it. If I ran, I would bring attention to myself. If I walked calmly, no one would have reason to suspect I was me. It would not cross most people's minds that you could be something other than what you were born.

I made it through our housing area and into town. I went unnoticed. There were no second glances. There were no jokes from the guard or tears from the children. I was just a Nit going about my business, and Nits had a right to do that. I still kept my head down, not uncommon for a Nit. After all, I was not presenting myself as an Ou. I would feel safer when I was out of our town, away from someone who might recognize me from the store.

I watched the Ous and the Nits and realized that I had taken off one costume to put on another. I was not a Nit any more than I was an Ou or a Travil. I was none, or maybe I was all, but this costume was a lot less confining.

MJ James fell in love with books at a very young age. Books were the one thing in the world that made sense and provided constant companionship. MJ was diagnosed on the autism spectrum at the age of 24. After their diagnosis, they went on to earn a BA in Psychology and an MS in Developmental Psychology. They are the parent of three incredible humans.

https://linktr.ee/mj_james

A.R.C. by L.L. Baker

Martha is the only human left on earth. ARC told her so. When she is seventeen, she will save the human race; she will become the mother of all humanity. That's what ARC has told her. There are only two more lights out until she is seventeen.

Martha's world is white walls and clean lines. She wakes each day to the bright light of ARC, hovering over her bed and playing what ARC has told her is bird song. She likes it; it's a nice way to wake up. Then she unfurls her body from the soft, paper-white sheets and scoots off the edge of her bed, feet dangling inches above the gleaming tiled floor.

Five steps to the bathroom where she relieves herself, she barely notices the small robotic arm that retracts back with her sample anymore. Then seven small steps and she is in front of the wardrobe. Martha is naked, as usual after lights out has finished. Her body has changed so much over the last few weeks, but ARC reassures her that this is normal. Her skin is a map of thin pink lines where she has grown so fast and so wonderfully. Martha peers down at them.

Then she is pulling back the wardrobe door and stepping into grey leggings and a grey long-sleeve top. Only two more lights out until she will save the world. Just two. She thinks on this as she sits down to meal one, holding out her arm for the blood pressure monitor and opening her mouth for the thermometer. There is a small prick on her outstretched finger; a droplet of scarlet blood blooms.

Martha watches ARC make a note of the readings, then a bowl of steaming porridge appears from a slot in the wall next to the table. It's topped with pumpkin seeds and chai seeds; a whirl of golden honey glistens on the creamy surface. She picks up the spoon that awaits her and tucks in. Martha is always hungry after the lights out time has passed.

"Tell me about the people again, ARC," Martha calls out to the white walls, and a screen appears suspended in front of her.

Images flash by and Martha knows them by heart. She mouths the words as a voice with no body tells her about the creators of ARC, about all the men and women who lost their lives in the Last War.

"Millions dead, humanity at the end of its existence—Abraham and Olivia Kenwell were commissioned by the world leaders to preserve humanity from itself. And so the Automated Repopulation Centre, or ARC for short, was born."

A light flashes above the screen and the images pause. Martha scoops the last dregs of porridge into her mouth and gets up. The bowl is retracted and a bottle of water appears in its place. Martha takes it, undoing the lid with a little crack as the seal breaks. The water is cold in comparison to the hot porridge, and it makes her chest feel strange.

Lights flash on the floor and Martha follows them down the long white corridor. She doesn't need to look at them anymore, as her feet know the way without her head. Instead, she clicks her fingers and the voice continues to tell her about Abraham and Olivia, about their daughter: Isabella. Martha has the same ash blonde hair as Isabella, that much she knows. But there are no mirrors in ARC. She has always wondered if they have the same face.

"After the death of Isabella, the couple made it their life's work to make sure that no other parent would have to go through what they went through. Life would carry on, no matter what humanity did to itself. ARC would make sure of that."

And so will I, Martha thinks to herself as she turns into the library. Here she clicks her fingers once more and sits down at the desk in the centre of the room. A curved screen flicks up in front of her and a woman with greying hair and bright red glasses beams down at her.

"Good morning, Martha." She smiles. "And how are you today?"

"I am well thank you, ARC," Martha replies, folding one leg underneath herself.

"I am pleased to hear it. Your body function results are good. Only two more lights out, Martha."

Martha peers up at the giant woman on the screen above her. She can see the lines around her eyes, the whiteness of her teeth as she smiles, almost as white as the walls of the Centre. Her mind wanders as ARC starts the lesson. Two more lights out. The time cannot go fast enough. Martha measures the time in blocks. First, there is meal one. Then lesson one: books and reading and general knowledge—she must be intelligent if she is to be the mother of all humanity. Then it is meal two. After this, there is exercise. Her body must be fit and healthy to carry the seed when it is ready. Finally, meal three, and after this is the time Martha longs for.

After meal three, she is allowed Free Time. This is the only time ARC is quiet. The only time she feels alone and unwatched. Another blood pressure test, another urine sample, and another thermometer and she can please herself. Her feet take her to the place she always goes, away from the sterile white of the Centre walls and the artificial light.

The biodome is full of green, every shade from lime to emerald. Martha loves the smell of earth and life. Here she loses herself in the swathes of ferns and towering sunflowers; she breathes in the blossoming jasmine and cups the soft petals of peach-coloured roses.

In the biodome, she can see the stars: the tiny pinpricks of light that bleed into the inky darkness. During lights out there are no stars, everything is just black and still. Out here her world moves. Nothing is clean and sterile and straight. Nature has no lines, just waves and curls and spirals.

Martha lies on the ground, her fair hair fanning out beneath her as she always does. Yet during this Free Time, she sees something she has never seen before. She sits up and stares.

The boy is standing at the edge of the biodome, where the white arc of the Centre is covered with ivy and moss and climbing, lilac-coloured wisteria. She has never seen another human before. She is the last human on earth. ARC told her so.

Martha opens her mouth to scream. She is the only one left. He cannot be here. But the boy quickly raises a finger to his lips. His eyes are wild and desperate, and Martha feels like they can see all the way into her soul. A soul is something ARC told her many people used to believe in; it's the thing inside you that connects you with God. It's the part of you that lives on after you die. Martha is sure he can see into hers.

His hair flops over his face on one side, and it is the same mixture of blonde and ash that hers is. The boy lifts one hand and beckons her towards him. Martha does not move. Her legs won't let her even if she wanted to. Instead, she looks at him as if he is a wild animal—a wolf out of one of the stories that ARC reads to her. A creature that might tear her limb from limb. That can never happen. She is important. But his eyes plead and she gets up.

"Martha," he calls. "Martha, come here."

Slowly, Martha puts one foot in front of the other. The plants and shrubs that once made her feel free are now closing in on her, trapping her here with this human where there should be none—just her. She stops a metre from him, close enough to see the details of his clothes: the strange symbols on his t-shirt and the heavy boots on his feet. Martha never wears shoes.

"How are you here?" Martha asks, fingers pulling at the sleeve of her top. She is bare. The thin material of her clothes seems inadequate under his gaze.

"It doesn't matter. You just need to know that I am." The boy pauses. "And my name is Oscar."

"But ARC told me ..." The words stick in Martha's throat, and she is suddenly very thirsty.

"ARC lied to you."

Martha shakes her head. ARC has no reason to lie. ARC is here to save humanity. She is here to save humanity. They are both here to do good, so why would ARC lie about that? Martha has watched the images of humanity before ARC, she has seen the way they hurt each other, the way they shed blood like water.

"I don't believe you. ARC cares for me. You are the liar." Martha folds her arms over her chest. "I am the only human left."

It is the boy's turn to shake his head. He reaches out for her and then lets his hands drop to his side once more. His eyes fix on hers, and Martha struggles to hold his stare. Oscar's eyes are so blue they remind her of the photos of Mediterranean seas ARC showed her once.

"Martha, we don't have much time left. You just have to trust me," he pushes. "How many lights out left?"

"Two," Martha manages to say. Beneath her skin heat is rising, her chest tightens. She can feel her pulse under the soft skin of her neck and raises a finger to touch it.

"It's okay, Martha. I want to help you, but you need to help me first," Oscar begins, but the gentle tones of ARC cut across him.

"Martha? It's time for lights out. Tomorrow will be the eve of something beautiful. Your moment has come. Where are you, Martha?" says ARC.

"Come back tomorrow," Oscar mouths.

"I am here, ARC," replies Martha, taking a step towards the voice. Then she pauses, turning to glance back at the boy, but he is gone. She notes that there are no footprints left behind as if Oscar were a phantom.

As Martha walks the long, bleached corridors of the Centre to her sleep pod, she can't help but think about Oscar. Whilst she brushes her teeth, she wonders if he was a figment of her imagination, and as she settles herself down under the freshly laundered sheets, she decides that he has piqued her curiosity enough that she will go back to that spot under the creeping wisteria. She has a plan.

*

Martha struggles to sit still while ARC takes her readings the next morning. She pushes the porridge around the bowl, sinking the seeds into the thick slop. She cannot keep her mind away from Oscar.

"One more lights out, Martha," says ARC as it clears away the half-eaten bowl. "Your body function tests are good. Are you not hungry?"

"I am just excited about tomorrow," Martha lies. It is the first lie she has ever told, and she wonders if it will be the last. There was something about the way Oscar's eyes pleaded with her during Free Time that she cannot shake. He was in her dreams, in that blurry bit between the end of lights out and waking. She could almost touch him.

Martha struggles through ARC's teaching. This time, it is about the seed, about how Martha will be put into an early lights out, and then the seed will be placed inside her—inside her womb. She rolls the new word around and around in her mind: womb, womb, womb. Her lips form each sound until it becomes strange to her ears. By the time she gets to second meal, not even her fingers can keep still. She still has exercise to get through.

She rushes through third meal, swallowing as quickly as she can, stretching out her arm so that her tests can be done as she eats.

"I am just so excited," she tells ARC, lying again. "Can I go for Free Time now? I need to unwind."

Martha forces her feet to walk, though they want to run, to skip down the corridors to the biodome. Inside, she lets herself go, crushing the delicate plants beneath her feet where, only the Free Time before, she trod ever so carefully.

"Oscar?" she whispers. Bubbles rise in her stomach as he emerges from the dark green cover. She reaches out to touch him, but he holds himself back. His eyes look sad.

"I'm so pleased you came," he says, smiling at her, but it doesn't reach his eyes. "I need you to do something for me."

"Wait," interrupts Martha. "Come and meet ARC. If it knows there is another human, then that changes everything!"

Martha can't keep her excitement in. It's like butterflies in her stomach, and she can't keep her feet still. They churn up the earth, the smell of it wafting up to greet her.

"If ARC knows, then you can come and live here with me. You can help with the seed. We can do it together. I am going to be the mother of all humanity. But it is lonely." Martha pauses to breathe. "Come on!"

"Martha, I can't. ARC can't know. I can't leave this spot. But I need you to do something for me. I need you to open the door," Oscar tells her. He folds his arms across his chest.

"The door? But you're already here."

"There are others, and we need to come in so we can save you." Oscar runs a hand through his hair. Martha thinks he must be about her age. She wonders what it would be like to run her fingers through his hair. She wonders what he smells like. All she can smell are the plants and the soil.

"It's dangerous outside. That is why I am in here. Safe with ARC," she answers. "Come and meet ARC."

She reaches for his hand, and Oscar tries to move away, but he doesn't quite manage it. Martha's fingers slip through his arm as if he were made of air. Her hand goes to her mouth, and she shakes her head.

"No," she mouths. "No."

"Martha, please. I am real. I am here. Please." Oscar's voice trails after her. There is pain in it as he tries to call her back without raising ARC's attention. His whisper is so much more deafening than any shout. But she runs. She cannot look at him anymore. He was the liar. He was a trick. Yet he looked so real and moved like the people she had seen on the screen. His chest rose and fell as he breathed in the oxygen around them, hadn't it?

Martha's footsteps slow as she reaches the edge of the biodome. She turns. He is still standing there, watching her, but the whole shape of him is deflated. It reminds her of a balloon ARC had once shown her images of. She falters for a moment. He mouths her name and presses his hands together as if praying before he drops to his knees.

Martha stands before him once more as he looks up at her. He slowly gets to his feet, brushing imaginary dirt from his knees. She doesn't know where he is or what he is, but he is different. He is intelligent, and he looks human. If she isn't alone ... If there is something in what he has to say, then she wants to know more.

"Where is the door?" she asks him.

***

Martha knows she hasn't got long before ARC calls lights out. She can feel the time slipping by. It has never felt like this before. Every section of time has passed in the way it is supposed to, ordered and planned. But now she is soaring off course, stepping away from the set path that has ruled everything between waking and lights out.

The door is at the end of yet another long corridor, one she has never been down before. She has never needed to, as it has never been part of her regime. Oscar has given her the code for the door. It changes every hour, so she has to walk quickly, but not so quickly that ARC will notice.

Martha reaches the door. It is the only one in the Centre. It is only her and ARC, so there has never been a need for a door. But here is one. Beside it is the keypad that Oscar told her about. Green and red numbers shine out at her as she forces her fingers to stop shaking.

Nine. Seven. Six. Five. Four. Zero. Zero.

"What are you doing, Martha?" ARC's voice stops her. She is one digit away from entering the full code. Her finger hovers over the number one.

Martha turns to face the empty tunnel. She would feel more powerful if she had someone to look at, someone to shout at, but there is nothing—ARC is all around, ARC is a safe haven, outside there is just death and destruction. Outside there is Oscar.

"Martha, what are you doing?" repeats ARC. Its voice is different. It sends a shiver down Martha's spine like needles.

"I am not alone." Martha stands up straight, her voice more confident than she feels. Inside she is trembling.

"You are the last human on earth, Martha. You will be the mother of all humanity. It is lights out now. Tomorrow is so special," ARC tells her.

When Martha feels the prick of a needle on her foot, she knows she is already too late. The darkness starts at the edges of her vision, slowly creeping in until the last thing she sees is the flashing keypad next to the only door in the whole of the Centre.

***

Oscar places the VR goggles back in his bag and slings it onto his back. He is no longer the seventeen-year-old boy he seems when speaking to Martha. His jaw is square, and a beard flecked with copper covers his chin. There are two others with him, just as there have been every time he speaks to the girl.

A man and a woman wait in the deep, dark, night. His skin puckers as he signals for them to make their way to their entrance into the ARC compound. There is a gap in the mile-high, barbed-wire fence, near one of the incinerator vents. Oscar has learnt not to hope, not to hold his breath as they sit waiting by the vent to be let in. Maybe this Martha will be different? Over the years, he has honed his words down to the ones that make her listen, the ones that set in quickly and make her doubt ARC.

As he yanks his bag off his back and squats down to push his way through the gap in the fence, he can feel the sharp corners of the photograph in his pocket. It has moulded itself to the shape of his body, but sometimes, when his senses are heightened, he can still feel it. Like now.

The three of them wait in the blackness. The incinerator hasn't fired up so that is a good sign. But Martha hasn't opened the door either. The one door in the whole of the Centre that doesn't lead directly into the government facilities ARC is attached to. The government facility who stole hundreds of thousands of frozen embryos for their "end of the world" experiment. The world never ended. The Last war had been painful, bloody, and long, but like all things it too had passed.

Oscar's legs cramp. He shifts his weight and pulls out the photo that digs into his thigh. There is a girl and an older boy, laughing and smiling up at him. One of them is Martha or, as she was known before all this, before she died, Isabella. The boy is himself, Oscar. He doesn't look at the photo very often, but it never leaves his pocket. He sees Isabella so often but it isn't her—not really. It is Martha, and Martha is different.

The morning light seeps through the covering of leaves that hides the three saboteurs. Oscar hasn't slept or eaten all night. The one door never opened. Martha either changed her mind or never found the door. Or, worse, ARC found her. Oscar winces as he pushes himself to his feet. They are numb and full of needles as they come back to life. The other two look at him for direction and he shakes his head.

"We come back tomorrow night. I'll speak to her again. She might survive," Oscar tells them, and they nod.

The three of them inch their way back to their entrance and shuffle through the gap in the wire. The walk back to their camp is quiet, their footsteps on the leafy floor the only noise in the still woodland.

Oscar thinks of his parents, of the things stolen from them: Isabella first, then himself when he joined the fighting, and their research on cloning and reproduction. They had seen the problems with ARC and had been in the process of destroying it when the government intervened. "For the good of the nation" they had told the Kenwells as they pulled files and memory sticks from the flames.

Oscar had returned to find his parents had filled their pockets with rocks and walked into the sea hand-in-hand when they heard he was lost in action. The government had made a mistake; they had sent officers to the wrong house, to the wrong Mr and Mrs Kenwell. He was never sure how much of a mistake it had been. The knowledge of ARC had died with his parents. The government had everything now.

Oscar returns to the ARC compound for the next three nights, donning his VR goggles and lurking by the incinerator vent. But he doesn't see Martha again.

On the fourth night, as he lifts his bag onto his shoulders, Oscar hears the roar of the incinerator, smells the burning flesh. It didn't work yet again. The stolen embryo was rejected by Martha's body. It either grew too fast, bursting through Martha's skin, or it didn't grow at all, rotting inside her, poisoning her from within.

ARC is clever. It knows success or failure within days. But for all the scientists the government has working on this hideous thing, they cannot work out how to create life. They continue to pump out clone after clone of his sister, each one just like the last. Grown in a matter of months in a strange orange liquid, yet this life isn't new. It's the same old life, repeated over and over and over. They are not God.

Oscar won't stop fighting them. He won't stop until he wins. Neither will the remains of humanity, which is camped out in the woods surrounding ARC. They didn't fight in the Last War for this. For their future to be stolen from them and frozen, for the men at the top to play God.

Oscar drops his bag and signals for the others to go back to their tents. They have time to kill now as the next clone is grown. In the dusky light, his eyes search for his tent amongst the hundreds that nestle between the tall, straight, trees. He picks up the pace as his wife emerges from beneath the heavy canvas. She looks up and sees him. Her eyes are tired, but she still smiles at him as he makes his way towards her.

Oscar reaches out for the bundle his wife cradles in her arms, and she relinquishes it with a gentle sigh. She presses a finger to her lips. He knows she was up all night, just like every night for the last few weeks. He peers down at the warm thing in his arms. She is sleeping now, but soon she will be screaming again for milk, for the smell of her mother's skin.

"Good evening, Isabella," he whispers.

He is fighting for her—for his sister and for his daughter. For every child, in suspended animation inside ARC.

As he watches his daughter sleep, he prays that the next Martha will be different, that she will open the only door in ARC and let him in.

Lydia Baker is an author of science-fiction and fantasy, she loves to write novels you can escape into.

Her novel 'The Return of the Queen' won the Pink Heart Society Reviewers Choice Award for Best Paranormal/Fantasy Romance in 2019 and 'Ava' was Shortlisted for the Agora Books - Work in Progress Prize in 2019.

When she's not writing she loves to read, to run and crochet (not all at the same time though!). She lives in Crawley with her husband and four children.

https://www.caabpublishing.co.uk

Radiation Days by E.B. Hunter

"Are you going to Jimmy's?" Stan asked as Max slid his radiation suit off its hook.

"Yeah. Just for a bit," he said, slipping the crinkly fabric onto his feet and hoisting it over his shoulders.

"You have your gloves? That suit's useless without gloves."

"I'm not stupid, Dad. I know what I need so I can go outside. Just because Mom ..." His eyes widened before they dropped to his boots. "I'm sorry, I didn't mean to ..."

It'd been six months since the blast, and Stan had decided to stay home with Max for a while. Just until school starts back up, he'd assured himself. His boss understood. The office would still be there when he was ready to go back. But Stan didn't know if he would ever be ready.

"It's okay." Stan cleared his throat, "Just remember to be SAFE."

"Yeah, yeah, I know. Stay Away From Everyone." Max rolled his eyes and put on his helmet. He twisted it and it clicked into place, latching to the jumpsuit. He went into decontamination room, closing the door behind him.

Stan stood at the small circular window, watching him exit into the outside world.

As the exterior door opened and the wind howled into the small space, he couldn't help reaching for his own suit, holding on to it just in case Max needed him. The door closed, and the room sealed with a hiss. Decontamination gas pumped in and lingered, blocking Stan's only view to the outside world, and his heart beat faster, sweat beading on his bald head.

The fans kicked in, and the mist cleared with a violent whirlwind. He could see outside again.

Max had made it across the road and to Jimmy's front door. The door slid open, and he disappeared inside.

Stan let out his breath, sighing like he had just finished filling in for Atlas, the weight of the world suddenly off his shoulders. He walked over to the B13 unit on the counter and punched in the code for straight black coffee. The machine whirred and ground up the organic waste in its basket, then sputtered hot black sludge into his Mickey Mouse mug.

He hated the mug. It had a chip on the lip that forced him to drink it left handed, and he had never been fond of the jubilant rodent. But it had been Deb's favourite. When he used it, he felt like she was there.

He sat at his cramped little desk in the corner of the living room and clicked on his ham radio. It's after three, Chuck should be home from the office now.

The electricity hummed through the old circuits, and Stan took a sip from the mug while he let the tubes warm.

He picked up the handheld and pressed the button. "Old MacDonald, this is Papa Bear. Are you in?" he said, using their code names.

The speaker crackled with static before Chuck replied, "I'm home Papa Bear. How're you and Baby Bear this evening?"

Stan smiled. Max hated that his code name was Baby Bear. "Doing fine. Just Papa tonight. Baby Bear's off with another cub."

"Oh good!" Chuck said. "I was hoping for some time to chat like adults."

"What'd you have in mind?"

"Well, I've been think—" the wind howled and shook the lead sheets that covered the house, and the lights flickered, making the radio cut out. "Anyway, that's what I've been thinkin'."

"Sorry, Old MacDonald. Wind blew you away there. Say again?" Stan crinkled his nose to push his glass up as he leaned in to hear.

"I said, 'I've been thinking about Deb' is all. I don't think that blast was an accident."

Stan felt the beads of sweat return, and he wiped his smooth head. "Wha-what do you mean it wasn't an accident?"

"Well, think about it. Has the warning system ever failed before?"

"Yeah. Once. When we were kids, remember?"

"I do. I lost my uncle in that radiation wave."

"I'm sorry."

"That's alright. It was a long time ago. Point being, do you remember what it was like before that 'warning systems malfunction'?"

Stan thought back. He'd been young. The first wave hit the Earth just before he was born. They had been lucky in America: it had hit the other side of the planet the first time. They'd been given time to predict the next radiation wave and shield their homes to protect their citizens. He still had nightmares about the pictures he'd seen in school that showed the devastation in Russia from that first wave.

"I guess we would've been about twelve or so? Things were pretty lean back then."

"Damn right. People were turning to cannibalism before they got radiated, things were so bad."

Stan grimaced, not wanting to think about the packs of waste walkers that roved the open country between cities. He didn't want to think about Deb like that. "What's your point, Chuck? Why don't you make your God damned point?"

"Take it easy there, Papa Bear, and don't use my name for Christ's sake."

"I-I'm sorry." Stan took off his glasses and pinched his nose to try and keep the tears back. "It's just, Deb. You know?"

"Yeah. And that's my point. Things were bad, then the warning system 'malfunctioned', and things got a whole lot better real quick."

"So you think they made it malfunction on purpose?" Stan felt his face flush.

"Your damned right I do." Stan heard Chuck's chair creak, and he imagined he leaned into the microphone. "There's been a lot of chatter on here. Lots of talk about food shortages. Not enough production coming from the cricket mines. Supply chains being hit by raiders. All in all, they figured there was only enough stock left for a week."

"A week? That can't be right."

"That's what I heard."

Stan took a sip of his coffee sludge and crossed his arms, letting the airwaves quiet while he pondered.

"Did I lose you, Papa Bear?"

He set the mug down and pressed the button. "No, I'm still here. You realise the implications of what you're saying, of course?"

"Course."

"I don't know. If that's the case, then why hasn't anyone else figured it out? Why isn't it in the papers?"

"You think they're just going to let people talk about it in public?" Chuck laughed. "No way, Papa Bear. No God damned way. They control everything! They deliver our food, determine our rations, what clothes we get. What jobs we do. Why on earth would they let us talk about this ... thing."

"The word you're looking for is genocide," Stan said.

"No. Not genocide. A cull."

Stan nodded to himself. "Yeah. I suppose 'cull' fits better." The wind gusted again, and the power flickered, making the radio squeal and turn to static. Stan took a sip of his coffee, his mind racing with the implications. Deb was gone, along with a hundred thousand others from the last blast. If this was true, then it would be the biggest cover up in history.

The wind slowed, and the power supply resumed at full capacity. "What do we do? How do we check this out?" Stan said.

"You don't 'check this out', Papa Bear," replied a thin, raspy voice.

Stan's stomach flip flopped, and he nearly dropped Deb's mug, splashing black coffee sludge on his shirt. "Who the hell is this? Where's—"

"Old MacDonald? Or should I say, Chuck." The man laughed. "He's"—a thump followed by a grunt came through the speaker from the background—"indisposed."

"I-Why are you doing this?" Stan said, trying to keep his voice level.

"You said it yourself, Papa Bear. It's a cover up. The squeaky wheel gets the grease. So, I suggest you stop squeaking or you'll end up like Chuck over here."

Stan's hand trembled, and he set the mug down before he dropped it. His arms felt numb, and he thought he might vomit.

The voice said, "By the way, thanks for the assist. We were having trouble figuring this 'Old MacDonald' guy out."

The line crackled and went dead, leaving the hum of the tubes and the ticking clock as the only noise in the living room. A room that had felt safe, and it now felt like a coffin.

The clock ticked out five minutes, one second at a time, before Stan could bring himself to switch off the radio. When he did, he felt an ocean well up inside him, an ocean he couldn't hold back. Is he really gone? Chuck...

The door hissed, and the contamination fans whirred. Stan took off his glasses and wiped his eyes, sniffing to hide the snot as Max came through the door.

"Hey there, buddy. Did you have a good time at Jimmy's?" he said, his voice distorted as he tried to make his face smile.

"Dad ... are you alright?"

"Uh." He coughed and looked at the mug on the desk, remembering how Deb worried about what Max found out about the harshness of the world. How she always tried to shield him from the horrors of the waste. "Yeah. I'm alright. Just ... just thinkin' about your Mom."

E.B. Hunter lives in a remote town in Northern Alberta, Canada with his wife and daughter. He spends his days working, and his nights crafting stories to entertain himself through the long, harsh winters.

https://ebhunterauthor.ca

About the Publisher

Writers Helping Writers

The Alliance was formed in 2022, and is a volunteer run, indie writer led organization. They strive to increase authors reach through community.

Read more at https://fsfwritersalliance.wordpress.com/.

Milton Keynes UK
Ingram Content Group UK Ltd.
UKHW010707220124
436466UK00007B/294

VERSUS

A FANTASY AND SCI-FI
WRITERS ALLIANCE
ANTHOLOGY

In this wonderful anthology from the incredible global talent in the Fantasy & Sci-Fi Writers Alliance, humankind is pitted against the odds.

Versus features thirteen stories that examine humanity's triumphs and failures in a world full of challenges. Drawing from science fiction, fantasy, ancient myths, and post-apocalyptic worlds, these tales examine the expectations and demands of society, love, death, and reality through the supernatural, the challenges of technology, and reimagined myths and legends.

Versus presents exceptional stories from:

MJ James - G. Clatworthy - EB Hunter
Kat Vancil - M. Fritz Wulderli - LL Baker
Isa Ottoni - SR Malone - EA Robins
Nick McPherson - Michael C. Carroll

ISBN 979-8-223-18348-8

9 798223 183488

Foreword:
Jade C Wildy
Edited:
Aaron H Arm